Nights At The Stray Dog Café

Don Nigro

A Samuel French Acting Edition

SAMUEL FRENCH

FOUNDED 1830

SAMUELFRENCH.COM
SAMUELFRENCH-LONDON.CO.UK

FOR PRODUCTION ENQUIRIES

UNITED STATES AND CANADA

Info@SamuelFrench.com

1-866-598-8449

UNITED KINGDOM AND EUROPE

Plays@SamuelFrench-London.co.uk

020-7255-4302

Each title is subject to availability from Samuel French, depending upon country of performance. Please be aware that *NIGHTS AT THE STRAY DOG CAFÉ* may not be licensed by Samuel French in your territory. Professional and amateur producers should contact the nearest Samuel French office or licensing partner to verify availability.

MUSIC USE NOTE

Licensees are solely responsible for obtaining formal written permission from copyright owners to use copyrighted music in the performance of this play and are strongly cautioned to do so. If no such permission is obtained by the licensee, then the licensee must use only original music that the licensee owns and controls. Licensees are solely responsible and liable for all music clearances and shall indemnify the copyright owners of the play(s) and their licensing agent, Samuel French, against any costs, expenses, losses and liabilities arising from the use of music by licensees. Please contact the appropriate music licensing authority in your territory for the rights to any incidental music.

IMPORTANT BILLING AND CREDIT REQUIREMENTS

If you have obtained performance rights to this title, please refer to your licensing agreement for important billing and credit requirements.

CHARACTERS

ANNA AKHMATOVA

ANDREY BELY/FIFTH SKELETON CLOWN

ALEXANDER BLOK/SECOND SKELETON CLOWN

LYUBOV BLOK

LILY BRIK

OSIP BRIK

NIKOLAI GUMILYOV/THIRD SKELETON CLOWN

TAMARA KARSAVINA

VELIMIR KHLEBNIKOV/WAITER/BEAR/FOURTH SKELETON CLOWN

VSEVOLOD KNYAZEV/FIRST SKELETON CLOWN

OSIP MANDELSTAM

VLADIMIR MAYAKOVSKY

VSEVOLOD MEYERHOLD

OLGA SUDEIKINA

BORIS TOMASHEVSKY/KONSTANTIN STANISLAVSKY

SETTING

A cellar in Leningrad, formerly and now again St. Petersburg, in September of 1941, during the Nazi attack on the city—years earlier, in the second decade of that century, the location of the famous Stray Dog Café, through the prism of which, with the help of Anna's memory and imagination, we will see also other places at other times. Right, a narrow flight of steps leading from above. Only Anna and Tomashevsky will use these steps. Everyone else appears and disappears from the shadows of the café, from just about anywhere else. The play moves fluidly from Akhmatova's present in 1941 to her memories and fantasies about her experiences at the Stray Dog and in the years after. Some of these things happened, some might have happened and some could not possibly have happened. Ideally, the entire theatre is the Stray Dog, and the audience are invited guests, surrounded by the action. There are tables and chairs, a little puppet theatre on a table stage left, and slightly raised inner stage within the larger playing space, on which are set a big kettle drum and an accordion which Khlebnikov will play. Once they're all on, most of the actors will remain onstage for most of the play, moving in and out of the shadows as needed, but still in the Café. But when the Skeleton Clowns take you out, you're gone.

Music: Francois Couperin, "Les Barricades Mystérieuses," played on a piano, off. Also, the cast will sing their own words to the traditional "Dark Eyes," "Kalinka," and "The Internationale." Music for "My Little Russian Sweetheart" can be found at the end of the notes.

For Tatyana Kot.

There is something terrible in the destiny of Russian poets.
— Nikolay Gogol

Poetry is
the most beastly
of all things.
It continues
no matter
what happens.
— Vladimir Mayakovsky

Russia is beyond all comprehension.
There is no way to measure her.
There's nothing like her. Don't try
to make sense of her. Just believe.
— Fyodor Tyutchev

ACT ONE

1.
The Stray Dog

(A September evening in 1941 in Leningrad, formerly and later again St. Petersburg, during the Nazi bombardment. Sound of sirens and bombs. A shadowy cellar. Round wooden tables and chairs stacked here and there, mirrors scattered about, and upstage a slightly raised platform stage. Two persons are staggering down the steps right and through a low doorway at the bottom. **BORIS TOMASHEVSKY** *(51), historian of Russian literature, and* **ANNA AKHMATOVA** *(52), Russian poet, still quite slim and beautiful. She will get younger, then older again in the course of the play.)*

TOMASHEVSKY. Down here. This will give us some shelter.

(As **ANNA** *passes through the doorway.)*

Watch your head. Are you all right?

ANNA. I have these questions for the moon.

TOMASHEVSKY. You're a bit disoriented, I think.

ANNA. The whole city is disoriented. People wandering in and out of my flat. They think it's the men's toilet. For which I can't really blame them, because that's what it says on the door: Men's Toilet.

TOMASHEVSKY. You were hit on the head by a brick.

ANNA. And they keep stealing my silverware. I've been hiding forks and spoons in my galoshes. And now the

7

soup tastes like people's feet. But what can I do? I'm a poet. Do they expect me to eat soup with my fingers?

TOMASHEVSKY. Well, there's plenty of chairs here.

   (*Sitting her down.*)

Just sit and be still for a moment.

ANNA. (*Popping right back up again.*) I have to sit in a drafty room, drinking vodka out of a thimble, with strangers tramping back and forth all day and half the night, and informers hiding in the damp behind the wallpaper like toads, writing down everything I say. Did you get that, comrades? Can you hear me well enough, you pathetic little weasels? Should I fart louder?

TOMASHEVSKY. (*Getting her to sit again.*) Try to calm down and sit still. You might have a concussion.

ANNA. Look at all the mirrors. I have lived in so many mirrors.

TOMASHEVSKY. It's all tables and chairs and mirrors. Whoever lived here liked to sit in the cellar and look at themselves. There's an old lantern. Somebody's been down here, having a little tumble, I'll bet.

ANNA. Violence and lechery. And betrayal.

TOMASHEVSKY. (*Going to light the lantern.*) I'll get us some light.

ANNA. That son of a bitch Kutuzov took my virginity like it was nothing. He was so handsome, so elegant, so cold, and completely self-assured. He frightened me to death, but I couldn't rip my soul away from him. I was poisoned for life.

TOMASHEVSKY. (*Holding up the lantern, looking around.*) This is an interesting place.

ANNA. The first twenty years we write ourselves a script, then spend the rest of our lives recasting and playing it over and over again.

TOMASHEVSKY. Not your ordinary cellar. Actually, it looks familiar.

ANNA. My father abandoned my mother. The man who took my innocence abandoned me. Now I expect to be abandoned. And when that's what you expect, that's what you get. And it makes me uneasy, waiting.

TOMASHEVSKY. There are birds painted on the walls.

ANNA. Birds on the walls?

TOMASHEVSKY. It's rather well done, too.

ANNA. *(Rising, examining the walls.)* Do you know what this is?

TOMASHEVSKY. Somebody's old wine cellar. But why they would paint birds on the walls—

ANNA. It's the Stray Dog. This was the Stray Dog Café. This place has been closed since the last war. Olga's husband painted those birds. I used to come here with my first husband, what's his name.

TOMASHEVSKY. Gumilyov.

ANNA. No. That's not it.

TOMASHEVSKY. Your first husband was the poet Gumilyov. And you need to sit down. You shouldn't be popping up and down like that until a doctor's had a look at you. Really, you're not yourself.

ANNA. I wasn't then, either. I've never been. Everybody came here. Mandelstam and Blok and Mayakovsky, and Meyerhold, and my friend Olga Sudeikina, and Tamara Karsavina, the prima ballerina.

TOMASHEVSKY. *(Managing to get her seated again.)* Sit down and try to relax. The bombardment seems to be letting up. You're right. It was the Stray Dog. But it's been closed up for a very long time. I know a doctor who lives not far from here. I'm going to creep out and try to bring him to have a look at you. Just stay here and keep still. All right?

ANNA. The best times I had in my life were at the Stray Dog. There was a gate you went through to come down those steps like descending into Hell. It was always thick with smoke and mystery and laughter and sex, and it seemed to exist so vividly in the present, but there was a timeless feeling here, as if you'd stepped into a vortex in which past and future coexisted. If you looked closely at the walls at four in the morning you could see the birds moving and the leaves rustling before dawn.

TOMASHEVSKY. That's fine. You look at the birds and I'll be right back. Will you stay here?

ANNA. Where would I go? There is nowhere else. This place is the center of the universe. At least it seemed that way to us.

TOMASHEVSKY. *(Looks at her, hesitates.)* Don't move.

(TOMASHEVSKY goes up the steps and disappears.)

ANNA. At night, when I drift off to sleep, I return to this place. I have come down those narrow steps so many times, through the doorway so low Stanislavsky had to take off his head to get through. Artists and poets and actors and dancers. They blocked up the windows to keep out the real world and painted harlequins and birds on the walls. It was Bohemian paradise. Everybody slept with everybody, and we told ourselves it was all right because we were different. We were artists. There were no rules for us. An extraordinary collection of drunkards and sluts who all thought we were geniuses, and some of us were right, but how unhappy we made each other. And yet I have missed it so desperately.

*(Sound of Couperin's "**LES BARRICADES MYSTÉRIEUSES**", played softly on a piano, off.)*

There was just that little stage there, but on stage or off, everybody was always performing. Somebody would play and Tamara would dance.

*(**TAMARA KARSAVINA**, a prima ballerina, appears, from the shadows, and dances through the cellar upstage of **ANNA**'s back, unseen by her.)*

She was so beautiful. Such a delicate creature, but strong. Dancers are surprisingly strong. And the only virgin in the place. They took bets on who would defile her.

(**MANDELSTAM** *appears from the shadows, watching* **TAMARA**, *with a bottle and glasses.*)

And Mandelstam would sit and watch and keep me amused with eccentric explanations of the Kabbalah.

MANDELSTAM. *(Sitting at the table with* **AKHMATOVA**.*)* Malkuth is the tenth sephiroth in the tree of life. But it does not emanate directly from God. It emanates from God's creation. We can only know the creator through what he's created, like mirrors reflecting mirrors.

ANNA. Mandelstam?

MANDELSTAM. Which is why we haven't got a clue what the hell he thinks he's up to.

ANNA. Osip, what are you doing here?

MANDELSTAM. I try not to ask that question because I'm not sure I want to know the answer. Malkuth is a portal, a port of entry to the tree of life. We enter at the roots, and make our way upwards, but most are devoured by squirrels along the way.

> (*Others have begun appearing, moving to set upright and arrange the tables and chairs.* **MAYAKOVSKY**, **OLGA**, **BRIK** *and* **LILY**, **BLOK** *and* **LYUBOV**, **BELY**, **KNYAZEV**. **KHLEBNIKOV** *has an accordion.* **TAMARA** *dances in the midst of them. Some are singing snatches of the songs we will hear later in the play, or speaking to each other in fragments of lines they will say later, a lovely, growing, cacophony.*)

ANNA. Osip, I don't want to be rude, but I thought you were dead.

MANDELSTAM. This is Russia. Everybody here is dead.

MAYAKOVSKY. *(Singing, as* **KHLEBNIKOV** *accompanies on the accordion, to a tune that can be found at the end of the notes.*)
COME TO ME, MY
LITTLE RUSSIAN SWEETHEART,
LET ME HOLD YOU
NOW BEFORE THE DAWN.

SOON ENOUGH
WE WILL BOTH
BE FORGOTTEN.
TIME WILL STOP—
AND THEN IT WILL MOVE ON.

EVERYONE JOINING IN BUT ANNA.

SOON ENOUGH
WE WILL ALL
BE FORGOTTEN.
TIME WILL STOP—
AND WE WILL ALL BE GONE.

MAYAKOVSKY. *(Tall, charismatic, up on the little stage, taking over, as* **KHLEBNIKOV** *continues to play quietly.)* All right, children. Get the furniture in place for the evening's orgy. In the temporary absence of Meyerhold, who seems to have been detained, and Stanislavsky, who's signing autographs and caressing buttocks in the kitchen, I will be directing, and since I haven't the slightest idea what I'm doing, you probably won't notice the difference.

ANNA. My God. It's Mayakovsky.

MANDELSTAM. Mayakovsky doesn't believe in God. He believes he IS God. He's a great communist, but he loves to be in charge.

ALL BUT ANNA. *(Singing as they finish getting the place in order.)*

COME TO ME, MY
LITTLE RUSSIAN SWEETHEART,
LET ME HOLD YOU
NOW BEFORE THE DAWN.
SOON ENOUGH
WE WILL BOTH
BE FORGOTTEN.
TIME WILL STOP—
AND THEN IT WILL MOVE ON.
SOON ENOUGH
WE WILL ALL
BE FORGOTTEN.
TIME WILL STOP—
AND WE WILL ALL BE GONE.

ANNA. There's Blok and his beautiful wife, Lyubov. And Andrey Bely. And Lily and Osip Brik. And poor, strange Khlebnikov, who was obsessed with birds.

KHLEBNIKOV. *(Having put down the accordion, and draped a towel over his shoulder, he has become a waiter.)* CAW! CAW! CAW!

OLGA. *(Spotting* **ANNA.***)* Anna. There you are. I've been looking everywhere for you.

ANNA. Olga?

OLGA. Where on earth have you been?

ANNA. I live in the Men's Toilet. I have spoons in my galoshes.

OLGA. What?

ANNA. I'm disoriented. I was hit on the head by a brick.

OLGA. Has Mayakovsky been throwing bricks again?

MAYAKOVSKY. I threw one brick, but, in my defense, I was aiming for Mandelstam.

OLGA. Gumilyov has been flirting with me shamelessly. You'd better watch out. I might give in. Unless I already have. I can't keep track. Oh, what difference does it make? Time is an illusion and one man is much like another. He courts you so desperately, and while you're making up your mind he wants to sleep with me. Of course, everybody wants to sleep with me.

MANDELSTAM. And everybody has.

MAYAKOVSKY. *(Banging on his kettle drum to get their attention.)* Ladies and gentleman, comrades, and whatever else might have wandered in out of the cold, let me welcome you to another night at the Stray Dog Café. I am your self-appointed master of ceremonies, Vladimir Mayakovsky, genius poet, genius playwright, genius painter, genius propaganda and advertising jingle writer, remarkably accomplished lover, street performer, carnival clown, prophet and pick-pocket, compulsive troublemaker and champion of the revolution.

MANDELSTAM. Nobody in the world has ever been as wonderful as Mayakovsky thinks he is.

MAYAKOVSKY. Tonight at the Stray Dog I am pleased to see several poets who are almost as good as I am: Aleksandr Blok, Osip Mandelstam, and my friend Khlebnikov, who is doubling as an accordion playing waiter, and appears to believe he is some sort of crow.

KHLEBNIKOV. CAW CAW CAW!

MAYAKOVSKY. And over here, the greatest living poet next to myself, the Empress of the Stray Dog, the ravishingly beautiful and mysterious Anna Akhmatova.

(Everybody applauds and cheers.)

First up tonight, a touching little tragicomedy entitled "Gumilyov's Proposal, or Love or Poison, Which is Better?"

ANNA. What is he saying? I don't understand what he's saying.

2.
Love Or Poison

(GUMILYOV *approaches* ANNA *from behind and speaks when he is quite close to her.*)

GUMILYOV. Why won't you marry me?

ANNA. What?

GUMILYOV. I said, why won't you marry me?

ANNA. Nikolay?

GUMILYOV. What's wrong with me? Am I not good enough for you?

ANNA. What's happening here?

GUMILYOV. I'm proposing to you again. That's what's happening. You ought to be familiar with it by now. I've lost count how many times we've done this.

ANNA. I'm very confused.

MAYAKOVSKY. Answer him. Keep the scene going.

MANDELSTAM. You'd better answer him or we'll never get anywhere.

GUMILYOV. Why won't you marry me?

ANNA. (*Finding herself slipping gradually into the persona of her younger self, and getting younger before our eyes, as if remembering somebody she was in a former life.*) I can't marry anybody.

GUMILYOV. Of course you can. It's easy. Why not?

ANNA. Because I'm not a virgin.

> (*Gasps of mock horror from the assembled onlookers.*)

TAMARA. So I'm the last one left in Russia?

OLGA. Apparently.

GUMILYOV. Don't be silly.

ANNA. I'm never silly.

MANDELSTAM. I'm silly.

ANNA. Mandelstam is silly, but I'm not.

GUMILYOV. You're just saying that to shock me.

MANDELSTAM. No, really, I am silly.

ANNA. I have no interest in shocking you. I'm a fallen woman.

GUMILYOV. You don't know what you're saying.

ANNA. I always know what I'm saying. Well, that's not true. Sometimes I don't know what I'm saying until I see what I write, and sometimes not even then, but in this case, I know exactly what I'm saying. Kutuzov took my virginity, and then threw me out like a plate of chicken bones. Nobody will want me now. I notice you're not contradicting me.

GUMILYOV. I am finding it difficult to speak. You must excuse me. I've just remembered some place I need to be.

ANNA. Where is that?

GUMILYOV. Not here.

> (**GUMILYOV** *goes upstage, gets a bottle marked XXX from* **KHLEBNIKOV**.)

ANNA. And then he went off and swallowed poison.

> (**GUMILYOV** *drinks the poison.*)

But unfortunately not enough.

MANDELSTAM. The only thing in his life he ever drank too little of.

ANNA. And a week later he was back.

GUMILYOV. (*Returning.*) Since the poison didn't work, and almost nobody worth deflowering is a virgin anyway, I have decided to accept you as my wife.

ANNA. Well, that's awfully big of you, but no thank you.

GUMILYOV. But I'm willing to forgive you for allowing that ridiculous, arrogant, unnaturally handsome bonehead Kutuzov to violate you. How can you play hard to get when I'm being so noble about this?

ANNA. I don't need your forgiveness. I've done nothing to you. I won't marry you because I don't love you.

GUMILYOV. That's all right. Nobody loves anybody as much as they think they do. You will learn to imagine that you love me just as I have learned to imagine that I love you, and we'll spend the rest of our lives imagining each other are very happy.

ANNA. And just who do you imagine is going to teach me how to do that? Love is not something you can practice like the piano. Either you love or you don't. And the truth is, I can't be in love with you because I'm still in love with Kutuzov.

GUMILYOV. But Kutuzov is a swine.

OLGA. That's always so attractive in a man.

GUMILYOV. I'll help you forget him.

ANNA. I'm a poet. I can't forget anything.

GUMILYOV. So you plan on suffering for the rest of your life?

ANNA. Basically, yes.

GUMILYOV. Then marry me, and we'll suffer together.

ANNA. No. I can't. It's absolutely pointless.

GUMILYOV. This is Russia. Everything is pointless. What's the real problem? It's not that some brain dead store manikin seduced and humiliated you. The person we think we love is just a peg we hang our delusions on. What are you really afraid of?

ANNA. That you will never shut up and leave me alone.

GUMILYOV. Besides that.

ANNA. That nobody will ever need me.

GUMILYOV. I need you. I'm somebody.

ANNA. Not really. I don't mean you're not somebody. I'm not sure who, because all I ever hear from you is that you love me, which means you want to sleep with me. You just want me because I won't have you. That's how these things work.

BRIK. Excuse me, but this is really not a very good scene.

GUMILYOV. What's wrong with it?

BRIK. I just don't believe it.

GUMILYOV. But it's what happened.

BRIK. I don't see what that's got to do with it.

GUMILYOV. Why do we let critics in here?

MAYAKOVSKY. No. Brik is right. Something is missing. What is it? A rocking horse? An actual horse? Where is Meyerhold when we need him?

BRIK. Meyerhold has been detained by the Secret Police. But I am assured by friends there that he'll be released soon.

MANDELSTAM. You have friends in the Secret Police?

LILY. In Russia, it's smart to have friends everywhere. And my husband is very smart.

MANDELSTAM. But it's not smart to be too smart.

OLGA. Puppets. This scene needs puppets.

MAYAKOVSKY. No. I'm sick of puppets.

OLGA. How could anybody be sick of puppets? Puppets are the secret of life.

KHLEBNIKOV. Birds are the secret of life. Maybe bird puppets.

OLGA. And they should play the scene naked.

TAMARA. You always want everybody to be naked.

OLGA. Everybody should be naked. Except Rasputin. Rasputin should not be naked. Although I hear he's got an enormous wart on his penis which increases sexual pleasure.

BRIK. Rasputin once tried to seduce my wife on a train.

OLGA. Did he have a wart on his penis?

BRIK. I don't know.

*(Turning to **LILY**.)*

Did Rasputin have a wart on his penis?

LILY. I didn't see his penis.

OLGA. You should have asked him to show you his penis.

LILY. I meet Rasputin on a train and you think I should ask him to show me his penis?

OLGA. Well, how else are you going to see it?

MANDELSTAM. From what I hear, Rasputin likes to show his penis.

BLOK. This is not about Rasputin's penis.

OLGA. Maybe it should be. There should be a scene about Rasputin's penis. We could do it with puppets.

BELY. She tells you Kutuzov took her virginity, you drink poison, and she is pleased. Is that right?

ANNA. I was not pleased.

OLGA. You were a little bit pleased.

GUMILYOV. At any rate, she changed her mind, and told me she'd marry me, and I was so excited I almost stopped sleeping with other women. But then she changed her mind again.

BELY. So she was playing with you.

ANNA. I was not playing with him. I thought better of it.

OLGA. You were playing with him a little bit.

GUMILYOV. So I took poison again.

OLGA. Couldn't you think of a more creative way to kill yourself?

GUMILYOV. Like what?

OLGA. Like placing your head under an elephant.

GUMILYOV. I didn't have an elephant. I had some poison left. I didn't want to waste it.

MANDELSTAM. Russian logic.

> (**GUMILYOV** *drinks from the bottle again.* **KHLEBNIKOV** *brings a bucket just in time for him to vomit into it.*)

ANNA. He got sick as a dog, but he still didn't die.

LYUBOV. So then you told him you'd marry him?

ANNA. I told him he should get better poison. The truth is, it was terrifying, to be loved so much. But the minute I said yes, he ran off to Abyssinia. What is wrong with men?

OLGA. Pretty much everything. That's why I prefer puppets. Sometimes I talk to my puppets, and they answer me in little voices. And you can put your hand up their ass and make them say anything you want.

MANDELSTAM. Just like Stalin.

GUMILYOV. This is 1910. Stalin hasn't happened yet.

KNYAZEV. It's 1913.

BRIK. It's 1930.

KHLEBNIKOV. *(Consulting his pocket watch.)* It's 1922. I'll be dead soon.

MANDELSTAM. In the Stray Dog Café, all times and places coexist.

ANNA. I think this is not really happening. Or it's happening, but a long time ago, and I'm remembering it imperfectly, like a dream.

BLOK. Like a palimpsest. An imperfectly erased wax tablet. You can see earlier layers through the holes.

MANDELSTAM. In fact, we do not experience things in sequence. There is an apparent sequence in which we appear to experience things, but even that is hopelessly compromised by memory and the distortions of perception and understanding created by desire and fear. It's a jumble of past, present and future, botched and piebald memory, a present which is gone before we've fully experienced it, and a future which, when it's become the present, turns out much more horrible than we imagined, imagination being that faculty which allows us to experience vicariously a variety of possible futures, which then blur into an imperfectly remembered and largely incomprehensible past which we access through memory, which is imagination polluted by experience, and then suffer again and again in the pernicious grip of a relentless and largely distorted nostalgia which is really, ultimately, agony. Only death can end this ridiculous clown show. At least, one would hope so.

TAMARA. I love Mandelstam. I never understand a word he says.

MANDELSTAM. It's the only way to stay alive around here.

GUMILYOV. We're like a traveling circus. Mayakovsky is the ringmaster.

OLGA. Clowns. We should have clowns.

TAMARA. I'm afraid of clowns.

MANDELSTAM. This is Russia. We have too many clowns.

OLGA. Time does seem a bit odd in this place. I remember things in a jumble of images. Warm rain on the roof. Something whispering in the ivy. A white hall of mirrors. Splattered blood and brains on rose pattern wallpaper. There's a dead man on the staircase. What was his name? Anna, what was the name of the dead man on the staircase?

ANNA. I don't remember.

KNYAZEV. Play the game or die.

3.
The Periodic Table Of The Elements

(MEYERHOLD appears. LYUBOV, very beautiful, preparing for her audition. TAMARA and OLGA holding her hands. MEYERHOLD stops to talk briefly with MAYAKOVSKY. BLOK and BELY, at another table, watching.)

TAMARA. Lyubov, Meyerhold is here. It's time for your audition.

LYUBOV. I can't do it. I'm terrified.

TAMARA. There's nothing to be afraid of. Except clowns. And bears. I'm afraid of bears.

LYUBOV. But it's Meyerhold. He's Stanislavsky's assistant.

OLGA. They both pee standing up, like every other man. Although I heard a rumor Rasputin could pee out his ears.

MAYAKOVSKY. Why were you so late?

MEYERHOLD. The Secret Police wanted to have a little talk. It was nothing. They get tired of playing with themselves. There's one more audition. Blok's wife.

MAYAKOVSKY. Why are you auditioning Blok's wife?

MEYERHOLD. It's a favor to Blok. Have you something against Blok's wife?

MAYAKOVSKY. No. She's lovely, but can she act?

MEYERHOLD. We'll find out.

LYUBOV. I am Lyubov Blok. I will be auditioning for the role of the Lorelei.

MEYERHOLD. Go ahead.

LYUBOV. Why am I so unhappy? Something whispering in my brain that haunts me. The air is cool at night. The Rhine flows along. On the mountain, the last rays of the evening. The Lorelei sits, combing her long, golden hair—

(**OLGA** *is combing her hair, humming the "Internationale" to herself.* **KNYAZEV** *watches* **OLGA**, *spellbound.*)

Her song casts an overpowering spell. In his little boat, the poet is filled with despair. Enchanted by the vision, he ignores the rocks below. The water swallows him up, poet, boat and all. This is how men see me, as some sort of enchantress, something not quite human, to be worshipped from a distance, even feared, perhaps, but never touched. As if to touch my flesh would turn them into stone. I don't want to be a symbol. And yet my fate is still to lure men to their doom.

MEYERHOLD. That's fine. Very good. Thanks for coming in. We'll be in touch.

BELY. *(To* **BLOK**, *as* **LYUBOV** *is hugged and congratulated by* **TAMARA** *and* **OLGA**.*) Here's the thing. I'm in love with your wife.

BLOK. Everyone is in love with my wife.

BELY. Except the difference is that I'm serious.

BLOK. This is Russia. Everybody is serious. But nobody is taken seriously.

BELY. You're not listening. I'm in love with your wife. I'm in love with your wife.

BLOK. All right. You're in love with my wife. We've been through all this before. Is my wife in love with you?

BELY. I don't know.

BLOK. So what do you want me to do about it?

BELY. You could kill yourself. It's a great career move for a poet.

BLOK. But if I'm dead, how can I sleep with my wife?

BELY. I can help you there. I'll sleep with her. Trust me, she'll never be lonely again.

BLOK. No. I'm not going to kill myself.

BELY. That's really inconsiderate of you.

BLOK. I'm a poet. We're very selfish people.

BELY. How many women have you slept with?

BLOK. I don't know. A couple hundred, I suppose.

BELY. Well, you can have all the rest. I just want your wife. That's fair, isn't it?

BLOK. You're a good friend, Bely. But not so good that you can talk to me like this.

BELY. Perhaps one day I won't just talk.

BLOK. Meaning what?

BELY. I could challenge you to a duel. You could die like Pushkin.

BLOK. I don't want to die like Pushkin. Even Pushkin didn't want to die like Pushkin.

BELY. But if a man is going to be shot, it's better that his best friend do it, don't you think? It's like shooting your horse. You don't want anybody else shooting your horse.

BLOK. I'm not your horse.

BELY. The horse is a symbol.

BLOK. A symbol of what?

BELY. That's the wrong question.

BLOK. What is the right question?

BELY. I'm in love with your wife.

BLOK. That's not a question.

BELY. No. It's not.

LYUBOV. *(Coming over to them.)* Was I good?

BLOK. You were wonderful.

LYUBOV. But I wasn't cast.

BLOK. You will be next time.

LYUBOV. No. There's something missing.

BLOK. There's nothing missing.

LYUBOV. Something is missing inside me.

BLOK. I've looked inside you. There's nothing missing.

LYUBOV. There is. I can feel it. I have empty spaces. Let's go home.

BLOK. You go ahead. I'll be along later.

LYUBOV. Not tonight. I'm cold.

BLOK. Let me go and talk to Meyerhold first.

LYUBOV. No. Don't. I don't want any special favors.

BLOK. Nonsense. It won't hurt to ask.

(**BLOK** *goes over to talk with* **MEYERHOLD**.)

LYUBOV. My father invented the Periodic Table Of The Elements. I wish my husband made as much sense to me as that does. How can he be so brilliant and so stupid at the same time? I reach out to him and he's gone.

BELY. Why don't you leave him?

LYUBOV. I'll never leave him.

BELY. Why not? You're very unhappy.

LYUBOV. This is Russia. Everybody is unhappy.

BELY. You and I could run off together.

LYUBOV. I told you, I'm not running off with you.

BELY. You said you loved me.

LYUBOV. I don't know what I said. I was very upset.

BELY. We were going to Italy.

LYUBOV. That was your idea, not mine. I was confused. I was unhappy. I was trying to make him jealous. I don't know what I was doing.

BELY. You know I worship you.

LYUBOV. I don't need you worshipping me. My husband worships me.

BELY. Then I won't worship you. I'll treat you very badly. I'll beat you. I'll sleep with other women. But then I'll come home and mount you like a horse.

LYUBOV. Well, that's very tempting, but no thank you.

(**LYUBOV** *turns and leaves him.*)

BELY. How does one cross the vast and bottomless chasm between the soul and the flesh? If there is another place, where is it? How can I touch it?

OLGA. Trust me, pal. You're never going to touch it.

BLOK. *(Returning.)* Where did she go?

BELY. She went away. She always goes away. What did Meyerhold say?

BLOK. He said it was good, and she's very beautiful, but he can't use her.

BELY. Why not?

BLOK. He says there's something missing.

> (**BLOK** *drinks.* **BELY** *looks across the stage at* **LYUBOV**.*)*

4.
The Raft Of The Medusa

MAYAKOVSKY. Do you know why I hate Blok's poems?

MANDELSTAM. Because they're better than yours?

MAYAKOVSKY. Because they're like telegrams from yesterday. So are yours.

MANDELSTAM. Yesterday hasn't happened yet. It's our job to create yesterday.

MAYAKOVSKY. That's mystical garbage. The only true art is improvisation. If you're not the future, you're the past. And if you're the past, you're already dead.

MANDELSTAM. And if we aren't dead, you'll kill us. God is entirely constructed of mystical garbage. That's the most appealing thing about him.

BRIK. God is like a jellyfish. In the air he turns to nothing.

MAYAKOVSKY. God is the past, and the past is something to be destroyed. The past is the enemy.

MANDELSTAM. You can't destroy the past. You'll keep making the same stupid mistakes over and over again. You've got to study the past, look at it with a clear eye, and salvage what's worth saving. The problem with Blok and the Symbolists is that they're so busy looking for some deeper reality, they ignore what's right in front of them, which makes for some lovely poems that don't really mean anything. Experience doesn't symbolize something. It IS something. The strangest thing in the world is what we actually see.

BELY. But there are layers of significance. Why refuse to see anything but the surface?

MAYAKOVSKY. The surface is enough to keep us busy without conjuring up a lot of hogwash about what's beneath it. We're tired of stumbling around in your stupid forest of symbols.

ANNA. But symbols do stand for things: emotions, psychological states. They're not mystical. They're more like a stream of fragmentary images we put together like a puzzle. I still think Blok is a wonderful writer.

LILY. So does Mayakovsky. He knows all Blok's poems by heart.

MAYAKOVSKY. Yes, but I'm trying to forget them. I don't mean Blok isn't a good writer. But from a political point of view his poems are pointless, pathetic, comic anachronisms. We Futurists love city life, machines, speed, absurdity, clowning, the inexplicable, the shocking. We hate tradition, sentiment, decorum, and the past. We've got to clean all this rubbish out.

ANNA. So I'm rubbish, too, am I?

MAYAKOVSKY. You are very beautiful and quite interesting. Every time I see you, you look like a different person.

ANNA. I am a different person.

LILY. When Mayakovsky is feeling lovesick, he reads your poetry. I think he's just a bit afraid of you. And germs. He's terrified of germs.

MANDELSTAM. Sooner or later, whatever it is you're afraid of comes and finds you.

MAYAKOVSKY. Mandelstam is afraid of me.

MANDELSTAM. I'm afraid of the consequences of your ideas. I find a bird in a cage in the attic and I want to write a poem. You want to strangle the bird and burn the attic. But if you burn the attic, the whole house goes.

MAYAKOVSKY. Let it burn. We can build a new house. All of Russia smells like moth balls. You Acmeists break with the Symbolists and discover you have no idea where to go from there, so you make up your own rules and then immediately violate them.

MANDELSTAM. What's the point of rules if you don't violate them?

MAYAKOVSKY. What's the point of rules? You find yourselves adrift in a life boat and after a while you begin eating each other, like the Raft Of The Medusa. The problem is, you're terrified of the water.

MANDELSTAM. Because it's full of sharks.

MAYAKOVSKY. The way to defeat sharks is to become one. And you want poetry to be rational, but your poems make no sense at all.

MANDELSTAM. It's the logic of unconscious association.

MAYAKOVSKY. In other words, you don't know what the hell you're doing.

MANDELSTAM. Exactly.

MAYAKOVSKY. Even Gorky is all worked up about protecting the art and literature of the past. Burn it all. It's like burning your prison. The best thing the Romans ever did was burn the library of Alexandria. What do we need with a few hundred more Greek plays? One new play that's honest is worth all that moldy old crap. Use and burn. That's life.

MANDELSTAM. In Russia the line between revolutionary and pyromaniac is very finely drawn. Destroy the past and you destroy yourself. You are entirely made up of the past.

MAYAKOVSKY. But what I am writing is the future.

MANDELSTAM. It's propaganda.

MAYAKOVSKY. But it's for the Revolution.

MANDELSTAM. No matter what it's for, propaganda is shit.

MAYAKOVSKY. But it's useful shit. It's fertilizer to grow the future.

MANDELSTAM. If you want a future that smells like shit.

MAYAKOVSKY. You'll see. The Revolution will change everything. And until then, we have the Stray Dog to shelter us. All of us orphans, huddled together in the basement of an old wine shop. Nobody owns us. Nobody claims us. We are the lost. But soon we shall be found. Or those of us who are smart enough to stay on the raft and not get eaten. And in the meantime, we copulate like it's the end of the world.

MANDELSTAM. It's the end of something. Bely wants Blok's wife. Meyerhold wants Yesenin's wife. You sleep with

Brik's wife. Olga sleeps with everybody. Tamara sleeps with nobody. And Anna is caught in between, making poems in the middle.

ANNA. Poems are better friends than people. It's always a mistake to love too much.

5.
The Terror Of Being Loved Too Much

LILY. I understand the terror of being loved too much. And also how something in us perversely resists the person we were born for. When Mayakovsky started dating my sister, I was horrified. He was so obnoxious. He would stand up at someone else's poetry reading and scream insults.

MAYAKOVSKY. MANDELSTAM IS A GENIUS, BUT HIS POEMS ARE AS DEAD AS PUSHKIN'S HORSE.

LILY. He made me so angry. I thought he was a hooligan.

MAYAKOVSKY. I am a hooligan.

LILY. He seemed so arrogant and insecure.

MAYAKOVSKY. Is it arrogant to want the future now? To want joy and love, now?

LILY. But you want everything.

MAYAKOVSKY. If you want anything you want everything. It's all connected. A future without joy is not worth having, and there is no joy without love. And you never have enough love.

LILY. Until you have too much, and then it's too late. But despite everything, when you stood in our tiny apartment and recited your poem to us, suddenly nothing else mattered, and my husband and I both fell in love with you.

BRIK. That is actually a rather stupid way to put it. But yes.

BELY. Love and envy and hate are all mixed up together in a person's soul.

BRIK. Is it permissible to want to destroy what one loves?

BELY. It's more than permissible. It's necessary. Otherwise, what would poems be about?

LILY. Of course, Mayakovsky and I were completely honest and open about our relationship from the beginning.

GUMILYOV. There's a recipe for disaster if I ever heard one.

BRIK. *(Waiting up for* LILY, *manuscript in hand.)* Oh. There you are. You're home rather late. I've been sitting here reading Mayakovsky's poems over and over again. They're so wonderfully brave and raw and odd and full of life. He's an absolutely unique character. I've simply got to publish them. I'll put up the money myself. He's really the most remarkable person.

LILY. Yes. He is. There's something I need to tell you.

BRIK. Have you spent more money on dance lessons? It's all right, although we might need to economize for a while so I'll have enough to publish Mayakovsky's book.

LILY. I've just been with him. With Mayakovsky.

BRIK. Ah. How is he? You should have brought him home with you. I can't wait to see him again. There's a great deal I want to ask him about his poems, and he brings so much life into our house. I'd give anything if I could write like that.

LILY. I've been with him.

BRIK. Yes. You said that.

LILY. He's in love with me.

BRIK. Well, of course he is. Everybody is in love with you.

LILY. And I'm in love with him.

BRIK. And who would not be?

LILY. I've just been fucking him most of the night.

>   *(Pause.)*

BRIK. Of course you have. Who would not want to?

>   *(Pause.)*

LILY. I hope that—

BRIK. So Mayakovsky is in love with you, and you're in love with him, and you've been fucking him most of the night.

LILY. Yes.

>   *(Pause.)*

You said you wanted an open marriage.

BRIK. Yes I did.

LILY. So it's all right?

BRIK. Why wouldn't it be all right?

LILY. I was thinking maybe he could come and stay with us.

BRIK. That's an excellent idea. We'll be working on the book. It will make everything much more convenient for everybody.

LILY. I knew you'd understand.

BRIK. So, should we get some breakfast? Or have you already eaten?

> (**LILY** *kisses* **BRIK** *on the forehead, then goes over to embrace* **MAYAKOVSKY**. **BRIK** *takes off his glasses and cleans them.*)

ANNA. Does it really not bother you, watching your wife with Mayakovsky?

BRIK. Lily has always flirted with everybody.

LILY. That's not true.

BRIK. You flirted with Rasputin on the train.

LILY. I wasn't flirting with Rasputin.

BRIK. Filthy fingernails, straggly beard, smelled like a goat. She's flirting with him.

LILY. He had very compelling eyes.

BRIK. The eyes of a maniac. Women like that. They're drawn to danger like flies to a corpse.

LILY. Rasputin actually looked at me. He almost looked clear through me. He paid more attention to me in five minutes than you do in five months. At least he was interested in me.

BRIK. Nobody in the history of the world has ever been more interested in anybody than I am interested in you. Mayakovsky, as I love you like a brother, let me give you some advice. Take all the joy in life you can, while you can get it. But if you ever feel the urge to marry, move to Switzerland and devote your life to collecting the labels off triangular pieces of cheese.

(BRIK moves away into the shadows.)

ANNA. Were you ever in love? You and Brik?

LILY. We were very young when we met. At first he wanted me and I wasn't interested. But then I thought about it and decided I was in love with him, and then he didn't want me any more. And I was destroyed. My hair started falling out in handfuls. Then he asked me to marry him. And I'd gotten over him then, and didn't really want to, but I heard myself saying yes.

TAMARA. Why, if you didn't want to?

LILY. I don't know why I do things. My emotions and my actions get out of step. One is ahead or behind the other, and before I know it I'm doing something I don't want to do with somebody I don't want to do it with, but I can't seem to stop myself.

OLGA. The secret is not to try.

LILY. The first year with Brik I was happy. Then he stopped sleeping with me. And when I asked him what was wrong, he said perhaps we should have an open marriage. So I started running around with someone to make him jealous, but he wasn't. He's the person I know best in the world, and he's a complete stranger to me.

OLGA. Sex is much better with strangers.

BLOK. Sex is always with strangers. Which is why I never have sex with my wife.

> *(BLOK drinks.)*

BELY. *(Looking across the stage at LYUBOV, as she looks at BLOK.)* The triangle is the most interesting of all the geometrical figures. There are many different kinds of triangle, but they all have three sides.

> *(KHLEBNIKOV on the accordion, a brief introduction, to the tune of "DARK EYES".)*

MAYAKOVSKY. *(Singing.)*
SLEEP WITH YOUR WIFE,
SLEEP WITH MY WIFE,

SLEEP WITH HIS WIFE,
SLEEP WITH HER WIFE,
WHEN YOU'VE RUN OUT
OF BETRAYALS,
PUT A BULLET
IN YOUR HEAD.

EVERYBODY EXCEPT ANNA. *(Singing, with* **MAYAKOVSKY**
conducting.)

SLEEP WITH YOUR WIFE,
SLEEP WITH MY WIFE,
SLEEP WITH HIS WIFE,
SLEEP WITH HER WIFE,
WHEN YOU'VE RUN OUT
OF BETRAYALS,
PUT A BULLET
IN YOUR HEAD.

> *(Some clapping, others whirling each other around
> in mad circles, wildly joyous singing.)*

SLEEP WITH YOUR WIFE,
SLEEP WITH MY WIFE,
SLEEP WITH HIS WIFE,
SLEEP WITH HER WIFE,
WHEN YOU'VE RUN OUT
OF BETRAYALS,
PUT A BULLET
IN YOUR HEAD.

> *(Big finish.)*

WHEN YOU'VE RUN OUT
OF BETRAYALS
PUT A BULLET
IN YOUR HEAD.

> *(Shouting at the end, glasses raised.)*

HEYYYYY!

6.

You've Broken Another Heart

(KNYAZEV approaches OLGA shyly, as KHLEBNIKOV continues to play very quietly. OLGA is putting clothes on a puppet.)

KNYAZEV. I love you.

OLGA. That's sweet. You're a very sweet boy.

(To the puppet.)

Isn't Knyazev a sweet boy?

(Answering as the puppet.)

Knyazev is a very sweet boy.

KNYAZEV. No. I love you. It isn't sweet. I love you.

OLGA. Thank you very much. I appreciate it.

KNYAZEV. Don't say thank you. This is not about please and thank you. I love you.

OLGA. That's nice, but I'm a married woman.

KNYAZEV. But you sleep with other people.

OLGA. So does my husband. So does everybody we know.

KNYAZEV. I don't.

OLGA. You were sleeping with my husband's lover a few weeks ago. And he's a man. Don't be unpleasant. We're put on this earth to enjoy ourselves. It's a sin to be unhappy. You're very nice but you're just a puppy, and I don't want you, and you won't want me either, once you've had me. Now, go, and let me talk to my puppets.

KNYAZEV. You have no idea. You have no idea what I'm feeling.

OLGA. It's not that I have no idea. It's just that I don't care.

(KNYAZEV watches her fuss with the puppet. Then he turns and goes to another table, sits, and begins drinking.)

BLOK. You've broken another heart.

OLGA. I'm teaching him about life. Sometimes it's kinder to throw the little ones back in the lake, at least once or twice. This is why I let the birds fly free in my apartment. You don't ever want to let yourself get trapped in somebody else's dream. That's always fatal to happiness.

BLOK. This is Russia. Russia is fatal to happiness.

(**BLOK** *looks at* **LYUBOV,** *sitting across the stage, learning her lines, while* **BELY** *sits close by, watching her.*)

OLGA. Trouble with your wife?

BLOK. My wife is never any trouble.

OLGA. Are you tired of her?

BLOK. I love my wife desperately.

OLGA. And she doesn't love you?

BLOK. No. She loves me very much.

OLGA. Then what's the problem?

BLOK. There is no problem. Except that I can't bring myself to sleep with her.

OLGA. Why not?

BLOK. Because she's a goddess.

OLGA. So instead of allowing yourself to be happy and making her happy, you've decided to drink yourself to death?

BLOK. This is Russia. Everybody is drinking himself to death.

OLGA. But you're a great poet. Even the other poets think so. And they all hate you.

BLOK. Writing does not make a person happy. Nothing makes a person happy but sexual intercourse, and that only briefly, and you pay for it with so much agony and humiliation that after a while it hardly seems worth the effort. This is the Devil's work, rummaging through the rubbish heap of one's life, looking for rhymes.

(**BLOK** *drinks.* **OLGA** *puts the puppet down, takes his hand.*)

OLGA. You don't need a goddess. You need a woman. Come home with me.

BLOK. You don't understand. I love my wife.

OLGA. You love your wife. But you need a woman.

(**OLGA** *kisses him, and leads him off into the shadows, as the others sing.*)

ALL BUT ANNA, KNYAZEV, BLOK AND OLGA. *(Singing, this time very tenderly,* **LYUBOV** *very sadly.)*
SLEEP WITH YOUR WIFE,
SLEEP WITH MY WIFE,
SLEEP WITH HIS WIFE,
SLEEP WITH HER WIFE,
WHEN YOU'VE RUN OUT
OF BETRAYALS,
PUT A BULLET
IN YOUR HEAD.

7.
The Curious Incident Of The Dog In The Night

BRIK. Possessive love is extremely foolish. If you love someone you want them to be happy. I love my wife. I want her to be happy. This brilliant hooligan Mayakovsky makes her happy. Why should I deny her this happiness? Some day we'll all be dead. Then what will it matter who slept with whom? All that will matter is that for a while at least one loved somebody. And if one was was loved in return, that is extra. We often sleep in the same room, two beds. My wife and I in one. Mayakovsky in the other one. The dog sleeps with Mayakovsky. Sometimes, in the middle of the night, Lily switches with the dog.

MANDELSTAM. The curious incident of the dog in the night.

BRIK. In the glorious future after the revolution, nobody will love anybody.

> (**BRIK** *finishes his drink and moves out of the light.*)

MAYAKOVSKY. He seems to be taking it remarkably well. Is he really not jealous?

LILY. I think he's a bit relieved. We haven't had sexual relations in a long time. So now he doesn't have to feel guilty about it. Do you remember the first time we saw each other? It was that night in the summerhouse. All I could see was the orange tip of your cigarette burning in the darkness. You took my sister into the woods.

MAYAKOVSKY. I wanted to show her the mushrooms.

LILY. In the dark?

MAYAKOVSKY. Mushrooms only grow in the dark.

LILY. You put on such a cynical front, but I could tell from the first you were sensitive and unhappy.

MAYAKOVSKY. Tell me about your wedding night.

LILY. My wedding night? What about it?

MAYAKOVSKY. I want to know what happened on your wedding night. Tell me everything. Don't leave anything out.

LILY. You want me to tell you everything about my wedding night with my husband?

MAYAKOVSKY. I want to know everything about you. Was it just unbelievably, unspeakably awkward and horrible?

LILY. Actually, no. It wasn't horrible at all. It was really very nice. He had spread flowers everywhere, and the bed was soft and smelled so clean, and Brik was a very tender and considerate lover. In fact, he can do things with his tongue that I would have thought only an aardvark could do.

MAYAKOVSKY. All right. That's enough.

LILY. But you said you wanted to hear about my wedding night. The truth is, it was very tender and passionate. I had several orgasms, and each time he entered me, I felt—

MAYAKOVSKY. Shut up. Just shut up. I don't want to hear it.

LILY. Well, what did you want me to say? I'm sorry my wedding night wasn't horrible enough for you. Would you like to write my lines out for me, so I'll be sure to say exactly what you want? As if this was all some sort of stupid play upon a stage?

MAYAKOVSKY. Why do you do this? Why do you torture me like this?

LILY. If you don't want to hear the answer, don't ask the question.

MAYAKOVSKY. You say you love me, but you never give all of yourself, and you always go back to your husband.

LILY. You want to possess me. You expect a woman to give herself completely and without reservation, and when she does, you lose interest, and treat her with contempt. Don't deny it. You've done it to a hundred girls. Like that poor girl who jumped out the window.

MAYAKOVSKY. That's not my fault. I didn't throw her out the window. And meanwhile you were off flirting with Pasternak.

LILY. I wasn't flirting with Pasternak. Pasternak was flirting with me. He flirts with everybody. Just like you. And I like his company. He's not so desperate as you, and I love the way he improvises. On the piano. I want to learn to do that. And I want to paint, and sculpt. And I want to take ballet lessons, and dance like Tamara and Olga. You are very, very important to me, but there's more in my life than just you. You need more love than anybody can give. Your need is insatiable and overwhelming. If you love me, let me be real. Let me be shallow and fickle now and then, like you. With Brik I was starving for love. But you're the opposite of Brik. Your love is so overwhelming I'll drown in it. At least Brik is realistic about these things. I don't think you have any business feeling contempt for him.

MAYAKOVSKY. I don't feel contempt for him. Brik is my friend.

MANDELSTAM. Your friend whose wife you're fucking.

MAYAKOVSKY. But it's all right with him. He said so.

BELY. Self-delusion is the key element in love.

MAYAKOVSKY. Why stay with him, if he doesn't want to sleep with you?

LILY. You're wonderful, but you're exhausting. It's such a relief to spend time with a man who is happy just for my company but can be alone without shooting himself.

MAYAKOVSKY. But that's not love.

LILY. Whatever it is, it's what I need.

(**LILY** *kisses him and goes.*)

MAYAKOVSKY. Sometimes I see myself standing outside myself, watching my performance. And I must say, I'm good. But not quite good enough to fool myself.

MEYERHOLD. It's better to stand outside yourself. The actor can't be trapped in his emotions. To destroy the false conventions of the present, we should embrace the false conventions of the past, and then subvert them. It's good to wear a mask.

MAYAKOVSKY. But when I take off the mask, what if I have no face?

MEYERHOLD. The mask is the face.

MAYAKOVSKY. You feel most at home on a stage. I feel most at home when I'm here, in a place that is largely imaginary. In this place, a person feels as if nothing can touch him. It's all inside a safe little bubble. But one day the bubble will burst.

8.
Some Day Our Poems Will Kill Us All

GUMILYOV. You're restless at night. I wake up and you're not there.

ANNA. As a child I walked in my sleep. On the roof, with the pigeons. Everybody thought I was strange. I swam like a fish in a thin dress that clung to my body and the boys all stared. Who cares what boys see? They're all morons anyway. This is my body, this is who I am. Everybody's free to look away. You're angry with me.

GUMILYOV. I'm not angry. I just don't like you prowling around the house at night. At four in the morning a woman should be in bed with her husband.

ANNA. I'm a poet. I get up and write. You run off to Abyssinia for months but I can't even walk in my own house? Why does a poet need to go to Abyssinia?

GUMILYOV. I'm gathering images for my poems.

ANNA. You don't need to go to Abyssinia for that. There's plenty of images right here.

GUMILYOV. Maybe for you. Not for me. Women are different.

ANNA. Sometimes I think you're jealous of my writing.

GUMILYOV. I'm not jealous. It's just that now they're calling you some kind of genius and it's hard to take that sort of talk seriously when you've seen a person naked.

ANNA. I can't help it if people think I'm a better poet than you.

GUMILYOV. Nobody thinks that. They just want to sleep with you.

ANNA. What a terrible thing to say.

GUMILYOV. Love is a terrible thing. When I took poison, I saw white shapes, and thought, this is death. Ghostly sheep in a blue field. Then I realized I was lying on my back in a cow pasture, looking at the sky. For a moment I couldn't imagine how I'd got there. Then I thought of you and remembered why I wanted to die.

ANNA. Well, if you get the urge to take poison again, go right ahead. I won't stop you.

GUMILYOV. I'll keep that in mind.

ANNA. I never claimed to be a genius. But a woman can be a genius. Tsvetayeva is a genius.

GUMILYOV. You're the opposite of Tsvetayeva. When she's hurt, she lashes out. She attacks the source of the pain, and becomes it. When you're hurt you build a wall around yourself, and force me to do whatever I can to break through it. Sometimes I think you have no real feelings at all. We're all just fodder for your poetry. In Egypt I had a long conversation with the Sphinx. She reminded me a great deal of you.

ANNA. Except I'm not made of stone. I have feelings. I tried to hang myself over Kutuzov, but the nail pulled out of the wall. Russians are not good at loving the right person. I think we're all suffering from a kind of sickness. The erotic, the mystical, the symbolic, the aesthetic over the moral, creation over compassion, indifferent to the suffering we're causing, oblivious to the consequences of our actions. There is a kind of sweet poison in the air in this place.

GUMILYOV. Why did you marry me?

ANNA. Your love letters were so beautiful. They made no sense at all, but they excited me so much I nearly went out of my mind. I could see the suffering in our future, but I moved towards it like a sleepwalker, eyes open, in the grip of some compulsion I didn't understand but had to obey. And even while you were courting me, you were sleeping with other women. You've never stopped.

GUMILYOV. Do you think I enjoy sleeping with other women? I feel it's my duty to you. The more women I have, the more poems you write, and the better you get. The problem is not that I don't like your poems. My problem is that you love your poems more than you love me.

ANNA. You betray me. They don't.

GUMILYOV. But they will. Some day our poems will kill us all. That's how we'll know they were good. Half the people who read them will want to screw us, and the rest will want to kill us. I haven't time to argue with you now. I'm going back to Abyssinia in the morning.

ANNA. Yes. That's fine. Run away. You'd rather go to Africa and chase hyenas and crocodiles than be with your wife.

GUMILYOV. The crocodiles don't get up at four in the morning to write poetry. In Egypt I'd make love to my mistress, then go out and step on tarantulas, and all the time I was thinking of you. I even tried to drown myself, but apparently despair makes you float. Will you give me a kiss before I go?

ANNA. Just stay away from me.

GUMILYOV. I'll give your regards to the crocodiles.

(**GUMILYOV** *goes.*)

9.
Everybody Here Is Mad

ANNA. If love is such a wonderful thing, why does it always leave me howling with grief and staring at the walls? Love is the Devil's poetry, scrawled on the mirror in blood. My father betrayed my mother and then abandoned us. The man who took my virginity dropped me before the blood was dry on the sheets. My husband runs off to Africa and I find pornographic letters in his desk from half the women in Russia. Now, when I am loved, it doesn't feel right unless it hurts. If I can't find a way to make it hurt, I move on.

KNYAZEV. *(Coming over from where he's been brooding and drinking.)* I can't believe she speaks to me this way. I know Olga loves me. Why can't she admit it to herself? What is she afraid of?

ANNA. You are the latest in a long line of fools.

KNYAZEV. Don't say that. I'm very unhappy.

ANNA. Being unhappy over love is a gigantic waste of time. Either a person wants you or they don't. If she doesn't want you, then move on.

KNYAZEV. I don't want to move on. I'm in love.

ANNA. This is Russia. Everybody here is in love. You'll get over it.

KNYAZEV. If it's love, you never get over it. That's how you know it's love.

(Holding his head in despair.)

It's true. She doesn't love me.

ANNA. I wouldn't let that discourage you. She doesn't love anybody. That's never prevented her from sleeping with whoever happens to be around at the time.

KNYAZEV. Don't say that. She is a good person. She's good and decent.

ANNA. She is pretty and charming, which unfortunately are not the same as good and decent.

KNYAZEV. She has a beautiful soul.

ANNA. Yes, and Blok is inserting himself into it even as we speak.

KNYAZEV. What are you saying?

ANNA. Olga is sleeping with Blok. Everybody knows it.

KNYAZEV. She's not. You're mistaken.

ANNA. She told me so herself.

KNYAZEV. That can't be true. Blok is much older than her. How could she sleep with Blok?

ANNA. She gets on her back and he crawls on top of her. Or he gets on his back and she sits on top of him. Or—

KNYAZEV. No. Stop it. I don't believe it.

ANNA. The real question is, why would Blok want to sleep with Olga, when he has a woman like Lyubov waiting at home for him? Of course, I heard a rumor that Lyubov was sleeping with Bely.

KNYAZEV. I don't believe that. Blok is Bely's dearest friend.

ANNA. And who in the history of the world has that ever stopped? Listen to me, you foolish little boy. You must learn this or you can't survive in this place. We always love at our own peril. The person we think we love is never the person they seem to be. It's all lies. Trust me. You must either learn to play the game or die.

KNYAZEV. Yes. Play the game or die.

> (**KNYAZEV** *goes into the upstage shadows and disappears. He will not return.*)

MANDELSTAM. What a cynical girl we are today.

ANNA. I'm just being honest.

MANDELSTAM. Yes, it's much easier to be honest about other people's loves than about one's own.

ANNA. My husband believes I have no feelings. The problem is not that I don't feel what other people feel. The problem is that I feel too much. I need to protect myself or I'll go mad.

MANDELSTAM. This is Russia. Everybody here is mad.

10.
Dancing Bears Drinking Vodka

MAYAKOVSKY. *(Doing a drum roll as he speaks.)* Attention comrades. The distinguished artistic hooligans of the Stray Dog Café have the great honor of being visited tonight by that legend of the Moscow Art Theatre, a man who inexplicably refuses to produce any of my plays, Konstantin Stanislavsky. *(STANISLAVSKY appears, a tall, distinguished looking gentleman. Applause and cheers.* KHLEBNIKOV *blows a duck call.)*

STANISLAVSKY. I would produce your plays if I understood them. I would even produce them if I didn't understand them if I thought they were any good. But as it happens, I have had instead the great privilege of bringing to the world the plays of Anton Chekhov.

MAYAKOVSKY. Which are garbage.

STANISLAVSKY. I beg your pardon?

MAYAKOVSKY. Chekhov is garbage. Beautifully written counter-revolutionary garbage. And I'm not the only one who thinks so. Anna agrees with me, don't you, Anna?

ANNA. No, no. No. Well, actually, yes.

STANISLAVSKY. You think Chekhov's plays are garbage?

ANNA. Not garbage, exactly. No, they're garbage. Everybody in his plays is so hopeless. In Chekhov, everybody behaves as if they're either constipated or on drugs. It's pathetic. But then, all of your productions are pathetic. No offense. Ordinarily I'd be more tactful, but I've been having a very strange series of hallucinations tonight. Maybe I shouldn't have been a poet at all. I'm double jointed. I could have joined the circus and been an acrobat.

STANISLAVSKY. Maybe it's not too late.

ANNA. All right. Chekhov is obviously not garbage. That was a stupid thing to say. I just object to the way he's held in such veneration by people who haven't got a clue what he was doing, or, for that matter, what you're doing. And what exactly are you doing? During *Uncle Vanya* I saw a mouse run across the stage, and the woman sitting next to me said, What a brilliant director Stanislavsky is. What immaculate attention to detail. Down to the last mouse. Do they really think you've been rehearsing the mice?

STANISLAVSKY. It took me months to train that mouse. It never quite got the hang of emotion memory.

MAYAKOVSKY. The mouse was the best thing in the production. No wonder Meyerhold hates working with you.

STANISLAVSKY. Meyerhold is like a son to me. He loves working with me.

MEYERHOLD. No. He's right. I can't stand working with you. It's nothing personal, it's just that everything you're doing is wrong. I realized it when I was playing *The Madman.*

STANISLAVSKY. A role you were born for. By which I mean you were very good.

MEYERHOLD. I was too good. I was mad.

STANISLAVSKY. You weren't mad. Your character was mad.

MEYERHOLD. I felt like I was going mad.

STANISLAVSKY. You were playing a character. You were lost in the moment. But you still knew you weren't mad. How could you have played the part if you were mad?

MEYERHOLD. Like a madman. You taught me to immerse myself in the emotion. And that's what I did. I felt the madman in me. And I don't want to be mad. And you pretend there's no audience. You can't act with integrity if you pretend there's no audience. If there's no audience, there's no theatre. The chemical reaction can only happen if you acknowledge, to yourself and to them that you know they're there.

STANISLAVSKY. I know there's an audience, in the same way you know you're not actually mad. What do you want me to do? Strut around like a clown, leering and smirking at them?

MEYERHOLD. You tell them don't talk, don't smoke, don't crack nuts, don't make rude noises. Let them make all the noise they want. It's our job to get their attention. How can we blame them if we're the ones who aren't doing our job? Did we pay them to come? Do they work for us? No. We work for them. Or we all work together. To find something together. It's their theatre as much as ours. Leave the doors open. Let anybody in. Theatre should be a kind of beautifully controlled chaos. Like the music hall and the circus. Mystery plays, farces and carnivals. Dancing bears drinking vodka. Clowns. There should be clowns everywhere. Experience comes to us in a jumble of strange fragments. And it's that strangeness out of which real art is made.

STANISLAVSKY. But our audience would hate that.

MEYERHOLD. Then let them hate it. Why should we expect everybody to like us? If half of them love us and half of them hate us and half of them don't know what the hell to think, it means we're doing our job.

MANDELSTAM. That's three halves. You're going to need extra seats.

STANISLAVSKY. I know what this is. You've always been terrified of your own emotions. Your sort of theatre is a retreat from honest human emotions into the safety of a kind of superficial second childhood.

MEYERHOLD. What if next time you cast me as a killer? What if I look for the murderer in myself and find him?

STANISLAVSKY. Then use it to play the role. That's your job.

MEYERHOLD. But what if I actually kill somebody?

STANISLAVSKY. You're not going to kill anybody.

MEYERHOLD. But how do you know? How does anybody know? There's got to be a better way to do it.

STANISLAVSKY. If there is, you're not going to find it by putting on a clown suit and running away from what's inside you.

MEYERHOLD. I'm not running away. I'm just going somewhere else.

STANISLAVSKY. Where? Where are you going?

MEYERHOLD. I don't know. I'll tell you when I get there.

STANISLAVSKY. Fine. Send me a post card. I'll be at the theatre, doing real plays. You can do whatever the hell it is you want with your clowns and acrobats and trained bears, but that's just not the sort of thing that excites me.

(*A large* **BEAR** *appears, runs up behind* **STANISLAVSKY***, stands on its back legs, and growls ferociously.*)

BEAR. RORRRRRRWLLLLLLLLLLLLLLLL!

STANISLAVSKY. (*Turning and seeing the* **BEAR.**) AHHHHHHHHHHHHHHHHHH!

(*The* **BEAR** *chases* **STANISLAVSKY** *all over the place, over tables,* **BEAR** *growling,* **STANISLAVSKY** *screaming, people running to get out of the way, some screaming, others laughing, rescuing their drinks just in time.*)

BEAR. (*Chasing* **STANISLAVSKY** *out.*) RRRRROWWWWWWLLLLLLL!

MAYAKOVSKY. I don't know. He looked pretty excited to me. Unless he's acting.

MEYERHOLD. (*Yelling after him.*) THE ONLY REAL PLAY IS A PLAY THAT DOESN'T TRY TO PRETEND IT'S NOT A PLAY. WE CAN ONLY GET TO THE TRUTH BY ADMITTING WE'RE TELLING LIES.

11.
The Puppet Show

ANNA. I agree with Meyerhold, at least about the fragmentary nature of experience. I knew a man who made mosaics. He put together an enormous number of little pieces and made them into something you could only see properly when you stepped back. A poet collects fragments of colored glass and constructs a labyrinth out of them in his garden, like an octopus. But if it doesn't begin inside you, inside your own soul, then how can it not be a lie?

BLOK. But what if what's inside you is a lie?

(Sound of a shot from off.)

MANDELSTAM. There's knocking at the gate.

BRIK. It sounded like a gunshot.

MANDELSTAM. They've begun shooting the poets. We used to meet in a tower. Now we meet in a cellar. Soon we'll all be permanently underground. But this is where I want to be when they come for us. At the Stray Dog Café, with Tamara dancing in a room full of cracked mirrors. What's the matter, little dancer? Are you sad tonight?

TAMARA. Do you see that man over there? That's Fokine, the choreographer. He's desperately in love with me, but mother made me swear never to marry a dancer, because she married one herself, and now Fokine won't speak to me except in rehearsal. The rest of the time, not a word. He just sits and broods. I don't understand this sort of emotion. Why should we cling to something that makes us so unhappy? My intention is not to break anybody's heart. My intention is to dance.

MAYAKOVSKY. Does it ever strike you how odd our life here is? We sit in the basement of an old wine shop, focusing on our own petty lives, while outside there's a storm brewing. Am I the only one who can see it? The storm is coming.

OLGA. *(Entering.)* We've had a bit of excitement. That boy Knyazev shot himself in the head on the steps outside my door.

ANNA. He shot himself?

OLGA. It made a terrible mess, too. I didn't think he had any brains at all, but clearly I was wrong. They splattered all over the rose pattern wallpaper. We'll never get it clean now. But on the bright side, it's inspired me to create a puppet show.

MAYAKOVSKY. *(Banging on his drum, as* **OLGA** *gets her puppets ready on her little stage.)* A puppet show. A puppet show. The actors are puppets. The audience is puppets. Everybody in Russia is puppets. And a foolish boy has shot himself in the head.

OLGA. *(Boy puppet on one hand, girl puppet on the other.)* Welcome to the puppet show. This show is called "The Love Suicide of Nevsky Prospect," a tragicomedy by Olga Sudeikina.

> *(Doing the voice of the boy puppet, holding a flower.)*

Oh, I love you so much. I can't live without you.

> *(Gives the girl puppet the flower. Voice of the girl puppet.)*

That's very sweet of you, but you must excuse me now. I'm going to go fornicate with an old poet.

> *(The girl puppet seizes a skeleton puppet and has violent sex with it.)*

Oh. Oh. Oh. Oh. Oh. You are such a great poet. Oh. Oh. Oh.

> *(Voice of boy puppet.)*

She is fornicating with my hero. How can she debase herself that way? Why doesn't she debase herself with me? I will kill myself.

(The boy puppet gets a toy gun, puts the gun to his head, pulls the trigger. **MAYAKOVSKY** *bangs sharply on his drum to*

simulate the gunshot and the gun squirts cranberry juice on the puppet stage wallpaper. As the boy puppet.) Help. I'm bleeding cranberry juice.

> *(Boy puppet falls. Girl puppet, looking down at the dead boy puppet:)*

Now look at the mess you've made. Oh, men are so silly.

> *(Girl puppet mocking boy puppet's voice.)*

I will kill myself. I will kill myself.

> *(Girl puppet's voice, picking up flower.)*

All over some silly idea you can own a person. If you want to be dead, be dead. That's your business. I want to dance.

> *(Girl puppet puts the flower on the boy puppet, singing as she dances:)*

SLEEP WITH YOUR WIFE,
SLEEP WITH MY WIFE,
SLEEP WITH HIS WIFE—

ANNA. Stop it. Just stop it. What's the matter with you? How can you be so cruel? That poor wretched boy killed himself over you on your own staircase and you make fun of him in a puppet show.

OLGA. Well, it's not going to hurt his feelings now, is it? This is what Russians do. We transform our tragedy into art. Or puppets. Or we just drink. I'm not the one who told him to play the game or die. I played the game. He died.

ANNA. It's true. I told him that. Play the game or die. Did what I said push him over the edge? And why did I say that? Was I just being selfish? Was I jealous? Or was I angry at my husband and all men? He came to me for comfort, and I helped pull the trigger.

MAYAKOVSKY. No. Meyerhold is right. This is exactly what's wrong with Russia. Too much sentimentality. I'm sorry he's dead, but, really, how stupid to kill yourself over a woman, when there's so many of them, and so much work to be done. And you're just as bad, to think about it more than it deserves. Look too closely at anything and first you get bored, then hypnotized, then depressed. I wrote that in a notebook which I was forced to eat when the Tsar's secret police came to confiscate our printing press. This taught me how useful art can be. I have subsequently eaten some of my best work and also a few things by Tolstoy. And what a humbug he was. We don't give a shit about the Kingdom of God. It's time for the Kingdom of Man. We will celebrate life, and work, and the revolution, and we'll fuck whoever we please. And any sentimental jackass who doesn't like it is welcome to shoot himself. Orgy after orgy. Then war. This is life. The art I want to make is the Art of Noise.

> (**MAYAKOVSKY** *bangs on his drum. Bang bang bang bang bang bang bang. But then, from off, the sound of shooting, several bursts.*)

BRIK. Listen. That's definitely gunfire. Somebody is shooting in the street.

> (*The* **BEAR** *runs in, stops center stage, and removes his head. It's* **KHLEBNIKOV** *in a* **BEAR** *suit. Sound of wind blowing. A storm outside.*)

KHLEBNIKOV. It's the Revolution. They're shooting in the streets. The Revolution has begun.

MAYAKOVSKY. THE REVOLUTION. THE REVOLUTION. THE STORM IS HERE.

> (*Singing, "**THE INTERNATIONALE:**"*)

RISE UP, YOU WORKERS FROM YOUR SLUMBER,
RISE UP, LIKE DEAD MEN FROM THEIR GRAVES,
OUR TIME HAS COME AND WE OUTNUMBER
THE PIGS WHO'VE MADE US SLAVES—

BRIK, LILY AND MEYERHOLD JOIN MAYAKOVSKY.

DON'T LET THEM SELL YOU THEIR TRADITIONS,
WAKE UP, AND HEAR THE BATTLE CALL,
THROW OUT YOUR WORTHLESS SUPERSTITIONS,

AND WE WHO WERE NOTHING SHALL HAVE ALL—
ALL BUT ANNA AND MANDELSTAM.
SO COME FORTH, COMRADES, MARCH,
AND THE LAST FIGHT LET US FACE,
THE INTERNATIONALE
UNITES THE HUMAN RACE.

*(Lights begin to fade as **MAYAKOVSKY** beats his drum as they sing.)*

SO COME FORTH, COMRADES, MARCH,
AND THE LAST FIGHT LET US FACE,
THE INTERNATIONALE
UNITES THE HUMAN RACE.

(Three last drum beats in the darkness.)

End of Act One

ACT TWO

12.
A Glorious Time In Mother Russia

*(As lights begin to come up, we can hear an accordion version of "**KALINKA**" and* **KHLEBNIKOV** *appears, playing the accordion. Followed by* **MAYAKOVSKY**, *and then gradually the others.)*

MAYAKOVSKY. *(Singing:)*

I'M RUNNING AND RUNNING AS FAST AS I CAN,
BUT AS FAST AS I CAN RUN, I CAN NEVER CATCH THE MOON.
BUT THE REVOLUTION'S COME, AND WE'LL ALL BE HAPPY SOON.
THE TSAR HAS ABDICATED AND HIS FAMILY IS DEAD.
TOOK HIS CHILDREN TO THE CELLAR AND WE SHOT THEM IN THE HEAD.

ALL BUT ANNA AND MANDELSTAM.

TOOK HIS CHILDREN TO THE CELLAR AND WE SHOT THEM IN THE HEAD.
WE'RE RUNNING AND RUNNING AS FAST AS WE CAN GO,
BUT WE KEEP STUMBLING OVER THE DEAD MEN IN THE SNOW.
FOR THE WOLVES COME TO GET US AND EAT US IN THE NIGHT.
THE WOLVES COME TO GET US AND EAT US IN THE NIGHT.

*(**KHLEBNIKOV** plays the slow, thoughtful quieter portion of the song in the background as* **MAYAKOVSKY** *speaks.)*

MAYAKOVSKY. Ah, it's a glorious time in Mother Russia. God, I love turmoil in the streets. I hear shooting, I run towards it. I can't get enough of the excitement. It's not violence I love. It's the pulsing chaos of people doing things. And there's so much to do. Everything belongs to the people now. It's the beginning of paradise on earth. I don't know whether to walk on the carpets or the floor, so I walk on the furniture. Soon we'll be walking upside down on the ceiling. I'm happiest when turning the world upside down. We'll read our poems with a grand piano suspended over our heads. Throw out Pushkin, throw out Dostoyevsky, throw out Tolstoy. Throw them all overboard and start over. In order to create, things must be destroyed. That's why I love Meyerhold. Everything Stanislavsky builds, Meyerhold knocks down. And I am the Playwright of the Revolution.

MANDELSTAM. The problem is, your plays stink.

MEYERHOLD. His plays don't stink.

OLGA. They stink a little bit.

MEYERHOLD. It doesn't matter if they stink or not. The playwright should just provide a rough scenario and then go away. We'll figure out the rest. Why do we need the author to tell us what to say? Now that we're in charge, no more authors. And none of that self-indulgent crap Stanislavsky calls honest emotion. Light and spectacle. That's what the theatre is. The author is as dead as God.

MANDELSTAM. Great. Let's all just grunt like monkeys.

MEYERHOLD. What's your concept? Concept is all. The only playwright I will allow into my rehearsals from now on is Mayakovsky. He's the only one of them who understands what theatre is really about.

MANDELSTAM. And he's insane.

BLOK. Stanislavsky wants the production to serve the author's vision. Meyerhold wants the author to be his servant. But why should anybody be anybody's servant?

Isn't that what the revolution's about? Meyerhold is brilliant, but in the future he'll be copied by morons who haven't anything like his talent, and when you take language and character out of theatre, no matter how well you do it, in the end, you make it less human, and more stupid. And what if comrade Lenin objects to what you come up with? What if he demands that you change it?

MEYERHOLD. Then we'll change it. For the good of the revolution.

BLOK. And then who is the servant? And who is the master?

MANDELSTAM. The problem with Mayakovsky's plays is that everybody in them is just Mayakovsky wearing a mask.

MAYAKOVSKY. And everybody in your poems is you wearing a mask.

MANDELSTAM. That's not true. There is nobody in my poems.

BLOK. And maybe nobody behind the mask.

MANDELSTAM. Just like that poor, washed up jelly fish, God, who's shriveled up to nothing. Your revolution is just a different form of religion. A fairy tale with an ever-receding pot of gold at the end. This horse is dead, so get another horse. The Tsar had Secret Police, you have Secret Police. They can change the initials and trade mustaches all they want, but when they're done with you, you're just as dead.

BRIK. It's useful for a poet to experience fear. The Secret Police provide a valuable service to the artistic community.

ANNA. Doesn't it bother you that your husband spends so much time creeping about with the Secret Police?

LILY. No. I like the Secret Police. The Secret Police are the servants of the people. Good people have nothing to fear from them.

BRIK. The soil of Russia is rich because it's saturated with blood. People deserve what they get. And they get what they deserve.

MANDELSTAM. Nobody deserves Mayakovsky's plays.

MAYAKOVSKY. My plays are just a spider web to catch more flies for the Revolution.

MANDELSTAM. You're a provocateur. A rabble rouser. An intellectual anarchist. They like you because they can use you. But don't delude yourself. When they've got rid of the rest of us, you're next. And Meyerhold, too.

MAYAKOVSKY. Poor Mandelstam. The noise and bright lights have brought on hallucinations.

MANDELSTAM. You're good at setting off fireworks. But it's all flash and very little content. And when the content you try to stuff into your work is propaganda, the result is simple minded idiocy. A poem does not comment on reality. It contains reality. It is reality.

BLOK. Reality is betrayal.

BELY. Reality is somebody else fucking your wife.

BRIK. Reality is a bullet in the head.

BELY. The Stray Dog itself is a question about reality. Nothing exists outside the Stray Dog, and inside it, all is fog. Out of the fog, into the fog. A sparrow flies from darkness into a brightly lit hall and then out the other side into darkness again. Blinding brightness, an incredible cacophony of sensations, then, before we can comprehend what's happened to us, back into the dark.

> (*The* **FIRST SKELETON CLOWN** *appears, a Clown with a skeleton mask, towel over his shoulder, like a waiter, brings* **MAYAKOVSKY** *a bowl of soup.* **KHLEBNIKOV** *is now sitting quietly by himself, brooding.*)

MAYAKOVSKY. You people see a waiter reflected in two mirrors and it's a mystical phenomenon, a doppelganger of some uncanny significance. I look at him and see my soup is here.

BELY. A waiter reflected in mirrors can signify much more than the arrival of your soup.

MAYAKOVSKY. I think the arrival of my soup is very significant. But I don't like to eat in restaurants. There are germs everywhere. I must have everything clean. My father pricked his finger with a pin and died of blood poisoning. The germs are always lurking, waiting to kill us. I love sex, but I wish it wasn't so messy. But then, everything enjoyable is dangerous. The imaginary God must have his little joke.

MANDELSTAM. The basis of humor is incongruous juxtaposition. Which is why sex is so funny.

OLGA. Maybe the way you do it.

ANNA. Sometimes it does feel to me like we're all characters in a play in somebody's head. Some insane god or poet.

MEYERHOLD. There is a kind of madness inherent in theatre. It's a game played with the spectators, with every kind of anachronism, dissonance, and eccentricity. The point of art is to make everything strange. To force the spectator to see things new. A play should be like a dance through a funhouse full of broken mirrors.

LILY. Mayakovsky, come and watch. We're going to dance.

MAYAKOVSKY. I've seen you dance.

> (*Turning to see* **LILY**, **TAMARA**, **OLGA** *and* **LYUBOV** *warming up and stretching.*)

Although I don't mind seeing it again.

BRIK. (*Spits in* **MAYAKOVSKY**'s *drink while his back is turned. Then:*) Finish your drink first.

> (*Holding up his own glass.*)

To the Revolution.

MAYAKOVSKY. To the Revolution. And to beautiful women dancing.

> (*Downs his drink.*)

ALL BUT ANNA AND MANDELSTAM. (*Singing.*)
> WE'RE RUNNING AND RUNNING AS FAST AS WE CAN,
> BUT AS FAST AS WE CAN RUN, WE CAN NEVER GET AWAY,
> FOR THE WOLVES COME TO GET US AND EAT US IN THE NIGHT.
> THE WOLVES COME TO GET US AND EAT US IN THE NIGHT.

13.
God Is Clever But Demented

(Sound of the Couperin. **TAMARA** *dancing, joined by* **OLGA**, **LILY** *and* **LYUBOV**.*)*

MANDELSTAM. *(Watching with the others.)* Now I am in the spider web of light. She will dance for me in the streets, in the white snow.

BLOK. I enter the dark church slowly. You change your shape as I gaze into the blackness. Neither dream nor reality, but something in between. God is clever but demented. His mind is a terrifying place to be trapped in.

TAMARA. Anna. Come and join us.

LILY. Yes, come join us, Anna.

ANNA. I don't dance.

OLGA. You used to dance. You were very good.

LYUBOV. Come dance with us. Please.

ANNA. Not tonight.

(Sees that **BLOK** *is watching her.)*

What are you gaping at? Are you in love with me, too?

BLOK. Everyone is in love with you.

ANNA. Only the wrong people.

BLOK. It is unspeakably painful for the soul to love silently. Am I quoting myself, or is it Tsvetayeva?

ANNA. Actually, you're quoting me.

BLOK. I thought it sounded better than mine. When I was young the world was a pulsing cryptographic labyrinth of symbols. Hidden meaning lurked everywhere, waiting to be revealed. Poetry was the key. Art was the means by which we discover the occult significance lurking in the visible. Lyubov was the luminous girl from shadowy chaos. The girl clothed with light. I had never seen anyone so beautiful. But on my wedding night I discovered to my horror that she was real. I desired her but at the same time I was disgusted. Body fluids. Flesh. Human scent. I fell into despair. I consoled myself with whores, contortionists and female acrobats. And finally she looked elsewhere for consolation. When she came back to me, she had somebody else's child in her, and I took her in. And I loved the child. But it died. The horrifying truth is, she is not a symbol of anything. The world is not made of symbols. Take away the stage sets and all you have is an empty theatre. Behind what we see there is nothing.

MANDELSTAM. But what we see is the dance, and the dance is very beautiful.

LYUBOV. *(Wiping herself off, coming over to* **BLOK,** *as the other three continue.)* I'm all covered in sweat. I'm tired. Let's go now.

BLOK. Let me finish my drink.

LYUBOV. You don't need anything more to drink. You're drinking yourself to death.

BLOK. But I'm not quite good enough at it, am I?

LYUBOV. Why do you spend so much time hiding in this place?

BLOK. I don't just hide in this place. Sometimes I hide at the theatre. Actually I hate this place. I've never even been to this place. I'm somewhere else entirely. I don't know where I am. It's all like somebody else's dream. Everything is emptying out of my head like sawdust. Look at Olga. She hangs her ex-lovers on the clothes line. They billow in the wind like old shirts. And it makes her so happy. I am not who you want me to be. When I was courting you, you were so cold to me.

LYUBOV. I was afraid of you. Something in your eyes. Something not quite sane.

BLOK. I come from a long line of crazy people who played the piano in the middle of the night. My father locked my mother in the closet and wouldn't let her eat. I'd never do that to you.

LYUBOV. And yet I'm starving to death.

BLOK. Bely is still in love with you.

LYUBOV. Bely is crazier than you are. Maybe we should just kill ourselves.

BLOK. You don't want to kill yourself.

LYUBOV. How do you know what I want? You look at me but you don't see me. You don't know me. You can't get past the outside. I live on the inside. First you seemed afraid to touch me. Then you attacked me like an animal. Now you can't stand to be near me. Just let me be your wife. I'm flesh and blood. I sweat like you. I feel desire like you. You're in love with somebody you made up in your head. And I'm not her. I'm somebody else. I don't know what. Maybe I'm nobody. And if I'm nobody, then where I belong is the theatre, where people who are nobody go to generate the illusion that they're somebody. But at the end of the day I'll still look in the mirror and see a stranger looking back at me. And I'll be alone. Remember the one who loved you. There is nothing else.

(LYUBOV goes. The dance ends.)

BELY. You've made her cry. You've made your wife cry. She just wants you to pay attention to her.

BLOK. I don't need to be patronized about what my wife wants by a two faced son of a bitch who pretends to be my friend while chasing after my wife and writing horrible things about me in the newspapers. I'll tell you a secret. All of us here hate each other. We're all competing with one another, always, for fame, power, women. We smile and laugh, make love, but we hate each other. And each of us will die alone. It's the monstrous truth that lurks at the bottom of the wine glass.

(BLOK drinks.)

BELY. I don't hate you. I love you. All right, I do hate you, but I love you more. I'm Russian. I don't know what the hell I'm feeling from one minute to the next. I just know that whatever I feel, I feel it passionately until I feel something else. That's better than feeling nothing, like you. You have the most beautiful wife in Russia and you spend your life drinking and sleeping with whores, sluts and lunatics. What the hell is wrong with you? She's a woman. She has the same number of openings in her body as any other woman. And you haven't just betrayed your wife. You've betrayed the Symbolists, too.

BLOK. The Symbolists? I've betrayed the Symbolists? Fuck the Symbolists.

BELY. And you've given lip service to a revolution you don't even believe in.

BLOK. It's true that I have been a willing participant in the events leading up to the present catastrophe. When the Revolution started, the first thing they did was burn my library. They are building the tower of Babel. Russia is a sleigh galloping blindly into the darkness towards the abyss. It is all a Russian mystery play. The Stray Dog is the whole world reflected in fragments of dark, broken mirrors. We are here waiting for the end of the world. We will die waiting. Everything will fade, become covered with ashes and blow away as dust. They call my poems dead rubbish written by a corpse, and it's true. I'm dead. All sounds have stopped. Can't you hear that there are no longer any sounds? The poet dies when he can no longer breathe. But if you die, it starts all over again. She has robbed me of my soul. She has sucked it out like the marrow from a bone. She has poisoned me with her kisses. I have gone mad from the poison. There is nothing. There will be nothing. Everything has already happened. Remember the one who loved you. There is nothing else.

(**BLOK** *staggers and goes out, helped by the* **FIRST SKELETON CLOWN.**)

ANNA. If you were really his friend, you'd go after him. He's not well.

BELY. You don't like me.

ANNA. It's not just me. Nobody likes you.

BELY. It's because I write horrible things about your husband's poetry.

ANNA. You write horrible things about everybody's poetry.

BELY. But you like it when I'm cruel. Because, in your heart, you're cruel, like me.

OLGA. Everybody is cruel, and everybody is kind. We get up in the morning, and look in the mirror, and ask, what mask shall I wear today?

MAYAKOVSKY. There is nothing behind the mask. There is nothing behind reality. What we can touch is our only salvation.

BRIK. What you think will save you always kills you.

14.
Never Look Directly Into The Mirror

(MAYAKOVSKY is pounding on his drum. LILY comes over to him.)

LILY. Do you have to keep pounding on that stupid drum? You're driving me out of my mind.

MAYAKOVSKY. I like rhythms. The rhythms conjure up the words. The sense comes later. What has Yesenin been saying to you? He had his face so close to you I thought he was trying to lick your nose.

LILY. He wanted to know why I'm wasting my time with you. He said, don't you know Mayakovsky's a joke? He's not a real poet. He's just playing one. He said he's a real Russian, but you're a fake. That in your heart you're some sort of American.

MAYAKOVSKY. He's jealous of my work. And he hasn't been a very loyal supporter of the revolution, either.

LILY. Oh, I don't know. He asked me if I thought you'd like to share me.

MAYAKOVSKY. Share you?

LILY. Since it's the Soviet way to share everything, he thought you wouldn't mind sharing me with him.

MAYAKOVSKY. That's it. We're going home to bed. I don't want you talking to that lecherous rustic smart ass any more.

LILY. I'll talk to whoever I want to. Don't expect me to give you everything, if you don't ask the same of yourself.

MAYAKOVSKY. I give you everything I have. I just occasionally also give it to other people.

LILY. Then so can I.

MAYAKOVSKY. It's not the same thing.

LILY. Why isn't it the same thing? Because you're a man?

MAYAKOVSKY. Because I'm the genius. I require a lot of stimulation. There are no rules for people like me.

LILY. There are no rules for me, either.

MAYAKOVSKY. But you're not a genius. You're the woman who loves the genius.

LILY. I don't want to be the woman who loves the genius. I want to be the genius.

MAYAKOVSKY. You can't just decide to be a genius.

LILY. Why not? You did.

MAYAKOVSKY. Well, you have a point there. Lily wins all battles.

ANNA. Between men and women it's always a struggle for dominance. There is no equality in love. Someone is always in charge, and it's always the person who's willing to lose the other.

MANDELSTAM. You realize that means nobody can ever be happy.

ANNA. What's your point?

MANDELSTAM. I'm a poet. I have no point.

ANNA. Mayakovsky has a point.

MANDELSTAM. Exactly.

BELY. In the future, art will consist of fragments of interwoven conversation, half remembered, misremembered, partially imagined.

ANNA. One should only write about what one loves.

MAYAKOVSKY. And if one loves nothing and nobody?

BRIK. Then it's time to shoot yourself in the head.

MAYAKOVSKY. No. The heart, I think. It's the heart one must kill. My goal has been to write things nobody would like, and I've succeeded brilliantly. I've offended the old and the young. Enemies and friends. I've even offended myself. Maybe it's time to go and stuff myself into the sausage machine.

MANDELSTAM. Mayakovsky, could you please shut up? You are not a Romanian orchestra.

MAYAKOVSKY. How do you know I'm not a Romanian orchestra? How do you know you're not a Romanian orchestra? Maybe everybody we know is a Romanian orchestra.

KHLEBNIKOV. God is a Romanian orchestra.

ANNA. I don't know what kind of orchestra God is. But I want to believe he's looking after everybody. Even us.

MANDELSTAM. Just not very well.

MAYAKOVSKY. God is an imaginary Romanian orchestra, and he's badly out of tune. Sometimes it's like I wake up from a trance and ask myself, who's been talking all this time? And if it's me, what the hell have I been talking about?

ANNA. Despite all his bombast and posturing, I think Mayakovsky is actually a very lonely person.

MAYAKOVSKY. It will be our little secret. Still, I'd rather be me than Mandelstam, who spends all his time digging into the petrified shit of the past, looking for truffles to put in his poems. But beauty will not save the world.

(Looking at TAMARA, who is wiping herself off after dancing.)

Although in her case, perhaps it can save it a little bit. Temporarily.

MANDELSTAM. You're right. I'm tired of fighting. Let's shake hands and be friends.

MAYAKOVSKY. I never shake hands. There are germs everywhere. They have little mustaches. They are invisible. Only Symbolists can see them. I'm afraid to touch anything.

MANDELSTAM. Except a woman.

MAYAKOVSKY. Especially a woman.

LILY. And yet you do.

MAYAKOVSKY. Because I love to gamble. Everything is a game of chance. Especially when it comes to women. But women are life.

GUMILYOV. And the purpose of life is to generate material for art.

ANNA. This from a man who's spent his entire life running away.

GUMILYOV. I'm creating a work of art about running away. My life is just research.

MANDELSTAM. Be careful while doing your research somebody doesn't take you out and shoot you.

BRIK. Mandelstam is right. You've been making sarcastic comments about the authorities and hanging about with the wrong sort.

GUMILYOV. What sort? Do you mean you?

BRIK. I mean one would be advised to be more circumspect. Just a friendly warning.

GUMILYOV. Well, nobody can see the future.

TAMARA. On Christmas Eve, if you put one mirror before you, one mirror behind you, and two candles in between, at midnight you can look into the mirror before you and see your destiny, if you can read it.

KHLEBNIKOV. Do you ever see me in the mirror?

TAMARA. No.

KHLEBNIKOV. Neither do I.

OLGA. I used to try to conjure up the image of my next lover. But you must never look directly into the mirror behind you, or you'll see your own death.

TAMARA. You don't look good. When's the last time you had something to eat?

KHLEBNIKOV. I can't remember.

TAMARA. Let me get you something.

KHLEBNIKOV. No. I'm having mystical visions.

TAMARA. What do you see?

KHLEBNIKOV. You.

LYUBOV. *(Entering, in tears.)* He's dead.

KHLEBNIKOV. Not yet. Soon, maybe.

LYUBOV. Blok is dead. I told him to stop drinking, but he wouldn't listen, and now he's dead.

(**OLGA** *and* **TAMARA** *rush to comfort her.*)

MAYAKOVSKY. Odd, that nobody saw that in the mirror.

BELY. This is terrible. You know that if there's anything you need, anything I can do. Anything at all.

LYUBOV. Thank you.

BELY. He was the best friend I ever had. He was like a brother. I loved him deeply.

LYUBOV. I know you did.

BELY. Let me take you home tonight.

LYUBOV. That's kind of you. I'll be all right.

BELY. Or perhaps you should just come home with me. Instead of returning to a place with all those disturbing memories.

LYUBOV. I'll be fine.

BELY. I'm always here for you. To comfort you. To care for you. I'd do anything for you. What do you want me to do?

LYUBOV. Don't do anything.

BELY. Now you can marry me.

LYUBOV. What?

BELY. Now that he's dead, you're free to marry me.

LYUBOV. Marry you? Your best friend in the world isn't even cold yet and you want me to marry you?

BELY. Well, you don't have to marry me tonight. I just don't think you should be alone. I should be there to hold you and comfort you.

LYUBOV. You want to sleep with me on the night of my husband's death?

BELY. I want to sleep with you every night of my life.

LYUBOV. But you're already married.

BELY. Not very.

LYUBOV. Get away from me. Just get away.

> (**LYUBOV** *goes.* **BELY** *stands there looking after her.*)

MANDELSTAM. I guess that's a no.

15.
All Men Are Insane

(Sound of a bell tolling, off.)

OLGA. So strange to think of all of us standing about like manikins in the rain at Blok's funeral. He'll be coming in the door again soon, of course. Here at the Stray Dog Café, the dead always return. It's one of the chief attractions of the place.

ANNA. From Blok I learned that it's the uneasy who write poems.

OLGA. He was a bit in love with you, I think.

GUMILYOV. He was in love with his wife. That was his mistake.

ANNA. Clearly all men are insane. Men I've just been introduced to hold my hand and tell me they want to marry me. I don't trust them and I don't like them. I fall in love with the worst of them instinctively. And they're always trying to kill each other. It's a pity they aren't better at it. But I create my own unhappiness. My loves are designed by some lunatic in my head to self destruct and generate the maximum amount of pain conceivable. Even when I'm throwing myself into something completely there's somebody in my head who's already withdrawing. I pretend not to love but do, or I pretend to love but doubt so strongly that I sabotage what could be happiness and gravitate like a sleepwalker towards despair. I'm drawn to what's hopeless and ignore what's possible. I have scripted an unhappy life for myself, those who love me and those I love, but for what purpose? So I can write poems about it? I enter into each new love as into a house of mirrors, with the dim awareness of betrayal to come. I don't want to be a reflection in somebody else's mirror.

GUMILYOV. Isn't my ex-wife magnificent? All these years and just looking at her still makes me want to kill myself. I was never worthy of her, but she stuck to me like a tick. She is prouder and more intelligent than I am. She seems fragile, but that's an illusion. She'll outlive all these dumb Soviet bastards. She'll exasperate them so much they'll drop dead of heart attacks and she'll still be there. There's a lot to be said for just being stubborn and holding on. I miss her every night.

ANNA. You were miserable with me.

GUMILYOV. Yes, but I was happy thinking about you when I was away. I was happiest during the war. I ate chicken, pig and goose until I was bursting, got drunk on plum brandy, and fucked everybody in sight. What a wonderful invention war is. But every second I longed for my wife.

ANNA. I was so glad when you came home safe from the war. I didn't want to be, but I was. And the first thing you did was jump into bed with one of Meyerhold's actresses.

GUMILYOV. Did I? Which one? Meyerhold has a large company.

ANNA. And then you ran off to fight again.

GUMILYOV. I asked them to stop the revolution long enough so I could sleep with my wife, but they were very unreasonable about it. Poets must fight, or they die.

ANNA. How could I have married a man who loves war?

GUMILYOV. War is life. You need to be near death to be sure you're alive. Take some pity on me. I thought I was getting a wife, when in fact I married a sorceress.

ANNA. I was not put on this earth to heat up your soup.

GUMILYOV. No, you can heat up the soup of that ugly Babylonian son of a bitch you're married to now.

ANNA. He's not a Babylonian. He's an authority on Mesopotamian culture.

> (The FIRST SKELETON CLOWN appears, looks across the stage at GUMILYOV.)

GUMILYOV. Do you believe this woman divorced me to marry a man who can spend all night blathering on about Assyrian pots?

ANNA. And all the while you were married to me you were still sleeping with Olga.

GUMILYOV. Everybody was sleeping with Olga. It would have been rude not to. How could I sleep with you when you kept me up half the night crying about some stupid puppet play?

>   (*The* **SECOND SKELETON CLOWN** *appears from the opposite side of the stage, looks at* **GUMILYOV**.)

OLGA. Everything is a puppet play. It's only stupid because everything is stupid.

ANNA. It's because a boy once killed himself over me, too.

GUMILYOV. Well, clearly he was better at it than I was. But you can't say I didn't try.

>   (*The* **FIRST** *and* **SECOND SKELETON CLOWNS** *move to* **GUMILYOV**, *put their hands on his shoulder, and whisper in his ears.*)

Yes. All right. You'll have to excuse me now. It appears I am late for my appointment with the Secret Police. Don't worry. I'll be back soon. Kiss the Babylonian for me.

>   (*Starts out, accompanied by the* **FIRST** *and* **SECOND SKELETON CLOWNS**, *turns back to* **ANNA**.)

You really are a wonderful poet, you know.

>   (**GUMILYOV** *goes, the* **FIRST** *and* **SECOND SKELETON CLOWNS** *on either side of him. Pause.*)

ANNA. Sometimes I see him smiling at me in the mirrors.

>   (*From offstage, the sound of a gunshot, loud.*)

16.
Pandora's Box

(As **MANDELSTAM** *speaks,* **OLGA** *is putting her puppets away in a little coffin-like box and the* **FIRST** *and* **SECOND SKELETON CLOWNS** *push out a coffin set on very squeaky wheels, pick up* **KHLEBNIKOV***, put him in the coffin, and close the lid.)*

MANDELSTAM. Two versions of Pandora's box. In each, she is curious, greedy, full of desire for knowledge, for experience, so against all warnings she opens the box, and all the evils fly out into the world—war, sickness, betrayal, death, and all that's left, at the bottom of the box, is one lovely, fragile butterfly, which is hope. In the first version, the butterfly hope is our salvation, a sign that redemption is possible, forgiveness is possible, love is possible. But in the second version, hope is the worst misfortune of all, because after immense suffering comes despair, and the quiet, level calm of those who have ceased to hope. But where there is still hope, suffering never ends.

(The **FIRST** *and* **SECOND SKELETON CLOWNS** *wheel off the coffin, wheels squeaking. Sound of crows cawing in the distance.)*

OLGA. Hope can drive you insane, but it's better to be insane than to feel nothing.

ANNA. I've done my best to feel nothing, but I've failed. When they took Gumilyov out and shot him, he had betrayed me a hundred times, and I felt terrible anger, at them, of course, but also at him, for being so reckless, and at myself, for not being enough for him, and also a sort of feverish lust, for certain nights when the sadness of sex—I can't explain it. I can write it, but I can't explain anything. And all explanations are lies. There is nothing but love, and that's a mess.

OLGA. But it's a lovely mess.

ANNA. And you're supposed to be my best friend, and you were sleeping with him.

OLGA. Well, you slept with him. Why shouldn't I?

ANNA. Why do you have to sleep with everybody?

OLGA. I am Psyche and Confusion. I'm the Queen of the Rainy Country. I am painted in various stages of undress. I act for Meyerhold. I dance Swan Lake. I impersonate the Madonna for Diaghilev. I am the girl with the Flaxen hair. Debussy dreams of me at night. I am the goat-legged nymph. I am the wildness and the terror. I dance like Salome with my lover's head and live in a house like a circus wagon, full of dolls and marionettes, with birds flying back and forth. There's a spiral staircase hidden in the walls so my lovers can escape from other lovers. But men are an illusion. Only women are real. Let's blame our fathers.

(Holding up the girl puppet and speaking in her puppet voice.)

Papa was a drunkard. When I was a little girl, I'd go to all the taverns hunting him, and drag him home. It's Daddy's fault.

ANNA. My father said the only difference between a poet and a whore is that a whore gets paid. He liked me when I was a little girl, but then he began to turn away. I don't know what I did. I don't know if he loved me. I don't know if he was proud of me. When he was dying I thought we could finally talk, but he kept seeing the Devil in the mirror. I told him, Papa, don't be afraid. There is no Devil in the mirror. And he said, I'm not afraid of seeing the Devil in the mirror. I'm afraid of looking in the mirror and seeing nobody at all.

OLGA. It is always a grave mistake to talk to one's parents.

(Putting her hand on ANNA's.)

I don't know why I do these things. I'm sorry.

ANNA. It's no use. I can't stay mad at you. And I'm no better. The horrible things we have done to each other in this place. The lies and betrayals.

OLGA. So here we are. They've shot Gumilyov. The Babylonian was horrible to you. I left my husband to live with a musician who invited you to come and live with us. And then he was sleeping with both of us. And now he's run off to Paris and we're left here alone with each other. Men really are pigs. Have you considered suicide?

ANNA. The thought has crossed my mind once or twice.

OLGA. I think about it quite seriously. I have a razor. And I have pills. And a rope. Or there's always Anna Karenina at the train station. I can't decide. It's like picking what dress to wear to the theatre. So instead I just drink a lot of vodka. I'm cold. Are you cold?

ANNA. So I've been told.

OLGA. But your poems are very passionate.

ANNA. Tsvetayeva's poems are passionate. I leave things out. Well, she leaves things out, too. But she puts more in. Do you think I'm cold?

OLGA. *(Touching* ANNA*'s neck.)* Your hand is cold. But you're warm here. Right at the pulse in your neck. I like to sleep with my puppets. Sometimes I think they're alive. But they don't keep me warm. For that, you need people. Or a dog. But I don't want a dog. They smell even worse than men. For company, I prefer birds. But you can't sleep with birds. Sometimes I wish I had a child. I have no child, so I must be a child.

ANNA. I have a child. But I know nothing about children. I sent him to be raised by someone else. I love children but I'm terrified of them. The way to have power over another is to never ask for their love. I have a history of driving away the people I love. I used to dance like you. Now I can only watch. It's like we're chess pieces, and somebody is playing us, and the chessboard is a labyrinth that leads to a ditch full of blood. We are dancing our way to hell. Why are you packing your puppets away?

OLGA. I'm going to Paris.

ANNA. For how long?

OLGA. For good, I think. I have no talent for going back. I burn my bridges while I'm still on them. If I stay here much longer, one day I'm going to meet myself in the street, and have no idea what to say.

ANNA. In Paris I sat on a bench in the rain in the Luxembourg Gardens under an enormous black umbrella with Modigliani. We wandered the streets at night in the moonlight like God's spies. I preferred to walk in the dark so people wouldn't gape at me. He painted me in the nude but I looked like somebody else. I was very happy there.

OLGA. Why don't you come with me?

ANNA. No. I can't.

OLGA. Come with me to Paris. We'll have fun, and we'll get away from all this horror.

ANNA. I need to stay here.

OLGA. Why?

ANNA. I don't know. Something is waiting for me here.

OLGA. Well, if you change your mind, you know where to find me. I promise not to write.

(OLGA *hugs her, gives her one of the puppets, and goes. She will not return.*)

ANNA. I have always been terrified of empty houses.

17.
The Island Of The Dead

BRIK. The secret is to forget what you want and focus on what is the case. At night I listen to them through the walls. Life is like being slowly devoured by rats. Rats inside my head, in my stomach. To watch another creature suffer. Is this part of the pleasure she gets when she betrays me? When I make others suffer, in some way I become her. I shudder like her. Union with the other through suffering.

LILY. Where have you been all night?

BRIK. I might ask you the same question.

LILY. You know where I've been. I've been with Mayakovsky. But I never know where you've been. Do you have a woman somewhere?

BRIK. I'm married.

LILY. So am I. But we have an open marriage.

BRIK. I'm aware that we have an open marriage. If our marriage was any more open, we couldn't recognize each other on the street.

LILY. And sometimes we don't.

BRIK. Sometimes we pretend we don't.

LILY. I never hid anything from you. I never hide anything from anybody. Which is why I feel perfectly free in telling you all about my relations with Mayakovsky. And you've been very understanding about it.

BRIK. Yes, I'm a very understanding fellow. I even go to court and defend prostitutes for free. But what I love most is working with the Secret Police. It's so good for one's character. Observing these interrogations eliminates the last drop of sentimentality in a person.

LILY. Do you like watching them torture people?

BRIK. Torture is a relative term. A person can be in agony just looking at his wife. Would you like some tea? I think we've got some arsenic left.

LILY. You're upset with me.

BRIK. Why would I be upset because the genius Mayakovsky is fucking my wife? He writes wonderful poetry and exciting plays and slogans for posters and he fucks my wife. Of course, I also fuck my wife, on rare occasions, at least once a year, when she's not busy, and sometimes when she's not there. But I write no poems. I write no plays. I write boring articles designed to prove that propaganda is art. I only connect to poetry through my wife when she's fucking the poet. Sometimes I have dreamed of choking you. Sooner or later the cuckoo comes out of the clock. Look over there, said Blok. Look the other way until you've forgotten what you love.

LILY. I'm sorry if you're unhappy.

BRIK. While you have been out fucking the genius Mayakovsky all night, I have been having a wonderful time with my friends, the Secret Police. You and Mayakovsky should come along some evening. It's really very stimulating. To know that, at any moment, if you choose, you could have absolutely anybody arrested, interrogated, tortured, and killed for absolutely no reason at all. Absolutely anybody.

(*Pause.*)

LILY. What is it that you want?

BRIK. I want you. I'm not jealous any more, but I want you. Or, sometimes, I don't want you, but I'm jealous anyway. How absurd all this is. The illusion of love. The humiliation of desire. But the sages who advise us to renounce it are full of shit. Desire is all we have.

LILY. Just tell me what you want.

BRIK. I want you to swear to me that you will never leave me. That you will never, never leave me. Swear to me that whatever happens, you will never leave me.

LILY. I will never leave you.

BRIK. Swear to me.

LILY. I swear to you.

BRIK. That you will never leave me.

LILY. That I will never leave you.

BRIK. Isn't marriage a wonderful institution?

18.
The Sky Is Weeping Uncontrollably

ANNA. In the festival of dead leaves, words from out of the darkness. A warm shower on the roof. A snowflake melting in my hand. The ivy whispering. A white hall of mirrors. I look in the mirror and see a strange girl, like a ghost in the doorway. God keeps poking at me with his fat, dirty fingers.

BELY. We communicate with God through piano improvisations and copulation.

BRIK. This is the sort of night when one must pay one's debts.

MAYAKOVSKY. Quiet, my kittens. A genius is speaking. Beautiful, melancholy Anna. If I was not so much in love with Lily, and with the Revolution, and with myself, I would pick you like a succulent fruit. Always writing poems about people's feelings. Write about something that matters. Of course, maybe nothing matters. God has oranges, cherries and apples, but everything in the garden has worms in it. We pop out of the jack in the box and then all go to the sausage maker. I'll wear a clown costume to my own funeral. I'm a hooligan like you.

ANNA. You're misquoting Yesenin.

MAYAKOVSKY. Yesenin belongs to the Revolution now. We can misquote him all we like. He cut his wrists, wrote a farewell poem in his own blood, then hung himself. It's a wonder he didn't eat rat poison and shoot himself just to make sure. I have no sympathy. A poet who kills himself is a traitor, both to poetry and to his country.

MANDELSTAM. Careful what you say. Some day you might want to cut your own throat. Then think how foolish you'll look when you're dead.

MAYAKOVSKY. And poor Khlebnikov, starving himself to death. Why does a man kill himself? Over a woman? It's true, the woman I love has been avoiding me. But do

I want to die? Sometimes. But I resist the impulse. As a political statement? What kind of political statement does it make to kill yourself when the government would be more than happy to do it for you ? Out of spite? Nobody cares. To boost his fame as a poet? That leaky ship has sailed long ago. Because he's ashamed of what he's done? Whatever he says is the reason, it's probably something else. A cold rain is falling. The sky is weeping uncontrollably. It's God, mourning his own death.The jackals come out of the woods at night and howl.

ANNA. Listen. I want to tell you something.

MAYAKOVSKY. That you secretly love me? That you want to run away with me and live on a chicken farm in Siberia?

ANNA. It's about the Briks. These people are feeding off you. They're too close to the Secret Police. You need to get away from them, before it's too late. They're going to eat you up like rats.

MAYAKOVSKY. You are speaking of my dearest friends.

ANNA. I am speaking of people who could get you killed.

MAYAKOVSKY. Nobody's going to kill me. Certainly not the Briks.

ANNA. Someone informed on Gumilyov. Someone could inform on you.

MAYAKOVSKY. That's ridiculous. Lily loves me. And Brik is perfectly happy with the situation. He believes in human freedom.

ANNA. And that's why he works with the Secret Police? Because he believes in human freedom?

LILY. *(Coming over to join them.)* If I want to find Mayakovsky, all I have to do is look for the nearest beautiful woman. They hang on his words like drool on a moron's chin. Although not the way they used to. I told my friend to write down everything Mayakovsky said because he's such a genius. She followed him around for weeks but he never said anything worth writing down. So to compensate her for her disappointment, I agreed to let her watch me take baths. Sometimes I let her sponge my back. You could, too, Anna, if you'd like.

ANNA. It's kind of you to offer.

LILY. I'm not kind. I'm generous but I'm not kind. Has Anna been trying to seduce you? Never trust a poet.

MAYAKOVSKY. She's been telling me how dangerous you and Brik are.

LILY. Well, everybody who's interesting is dangerous. Stalin is very interesting. Maybe I don't want Anna to wash my back. Maybe I'd better not turn my back on her. Because of how interesting she is.

TAMARA. Anna, come and dance with me.

ANNA. I don't want to dance.

LILY. Anna is afraid to dance.

TAMARA. *(Pulling* ANNA *away by the arm.)* Come on. I'll show you what Fokine and I've been working on.

> *(To* ANNA, *after she's got her away from them.)*

You need to be careful what you say to her. It's dangerous.

LILY. So Anna's been warning you about me, has she?

MAYAKOVSKY. I haven't seen you in days. Where have you been?

LILY. Spending a little time with my husband.

MAYAKOVSKY. So you'd rather be with him than with me now?

LILY. I need different things from different people at different times. He's a real person who listens to me when I talk to him.

MAYAKOVSKY. I listen to you.

LILY. You don't listen to anybody but yourself. You're an enormous baby. You're selfish and vain and dishonest. At your lecture, you stole Brik's stories about his life in Berlin and told them as if they'd happened to you.

MAYAKOVSKY. He didn't care.

LILY. How do you know he didn't care? Just because you say everything that pops into your head doesn't mean that he does. You think everything is simple. You have easy answers for everything. But it doesn't work that way.

MAYAKOVSKY. Have you been sleeping with him?

LILY. Who I sleep with is none of your business.

MAYAKOVSKY. I'm happy to tell you who I sleep with.

LILY. I don't want to know who you sleep with.

MAYAKOVSKY. I only sleep with the others because you won't leave your husband. The only one I want is you.

LILY. I don't see why it matters to you. You got just what you wanted. You got the revolution. And you're the most famous poet in Russia.

MAYAKOVSKY. But they want me to keep writing the same thing over and over. When I try something new they attack me like rabid dogs. I don't need a committee of ignorant, small-minded party jackasses to tell me what I can write. What I need is you.

LILY. I'm going to Berlin with Brik.

MAYAKOVSKY. I need you here.

LILY. Well, I need to be somewhere else, and what I need is what matters. I'm in charge of my own life. If you can't deal with that, then maybe we should be away from each other more often. You live in the future. I live in the moment. I'm sorry if the future has become the wrong moment for you. I can't help that. Just write your slogans for the party and sleep with your French whores. We'll send you a post card from Berlin.

(**LILY** *goes off into the shadows. She will not return.*)

MAYAKOVSKY. Shoot the clown in the head and cranberry juice comes squirting out. She is playing a sinister polka in my brain.

(**MAYAKOVSKY** *drinks.*)

A slap in the face of public taste. That's what I am. When did I become a flying prehistoric lizard? God help a poet who has outlived his usefulness.

MANDELSTAM. No poet ever outlives his usefulness because all poetry is useless. Except that without it, so is everything else. It is all made of loneliness, really. We do this because we're lonely. All of us live in chaos here. A monstrous, evil system of human enslavement has been destroyed and replaced by another monstrous, evil system of human enslavement. You were tolerated when you were useful to them. Now you're becoming a source of concern. Welcome to the club.

MAYAKOVSKY. The world is leaking. The Devil is eating the moon. God lives at Luna Park. He's the fellow on stilts, with roller skates. Acrobats and roller coasters are the secret of life. I am the Jack of Diamonds and you are all playing cards. We are sailing to the island of the dead. Pushkin? Throw him overboard. Dostoyevsky? Overboard. Tolstoy? Overboard. Mayakovsky? Overboard. There is no room for them on this Ship of Fools.

MANDELSTAM. You need to calm down. They're always listening now.

MAYAKOVSKY. I don't care if those dumb fuckers are listening or not. I am the last poet. I'd rather be on the street selling pretzels than play their stupid game. These people have milked me like a cow. I am the bells on the dunce cap of God. They've got me writing advertisements for pacifiers. I made posters that said, There is nothing better for sucking. You can suck this until you're dead. This fellow who had such contempt for rules and regulations and hierarchies has become the poster boy for them. We are all dolls and puppets now. All that has become of our glorious revolution is a nation run by puppets under the head puppet, who is a homicidal maniac. I have been playing a character with my own name. What will happen to me when he dies?

MANDELSTAM. Art is a dangerous thing. They're right about that. Objects, when paid attention to, take on unexpected significance. They don't like that.

(*Watching* **BRIK** *approach.*)

Be careful now. The Devil appears in the form of a critic.

(*To* **BRIK**.)

You can suck this until you're dead.

BRIK. I beg your pardon?

MANDELSTAM. I was just quoting Comrade Stalin's favorite poet.

(**MANDELSTAM** *goes.*)

BRIK. He's a strange little man, isn't he?

MAYAKOVSKY. I like him very much. I've come to like him more and more.

BRIK. We're keeping a close eye on him. There are enemies everywhere now. In my work with the Secret Police I have watched with increasing interest the torture of a great variety of criminals, and I must confess, on occasion I have actually taken a certain amount of pleasure in this. Some of them, I'm sorry to say, I once considered my friends. I think I might enjoy watching that one suffer.

MAYAKOVSKY. Do you consider me your friend?

BRIK. What kind of question is that?

MAYAKOVSKY. Why are you my friend?

BRIK. Why am I your friend?

MAYAKOVSKY. I'm fucking your wife. Why are you my friend? No more bullshit. Tell me the truth for once.

BRIK. Let us imagine that those above him have made it clear to a man that his duty to the party is to keep the celebrated poet of the revolution happy at any cost.

MAYAKOVSKY. You were assigned to inform on me?

BRIK. To keep an eye on you. To make sure you don't veer too far from the party line. Isn't that funny? We have banned irony from literature now, but my duty to the party was to be the best friend of the man who fucks my wife.

MAYAKOVSKY. You're telling me that all of these years, when I thought you were my friend—

BRIK. I am your friend. I'm your very best friend in all the world. And perhaps the only person left who really loves you.

MAYAKOVSKY. You've been spying on me. All this time you've been spying on me.

BRIK. It's never been a question of spying. You've been extremely valuable to the party. But you're erratic. You have individualistic tendencies. You needed someone at your side to quietly help guide you.

MAYAKOVSKY. How could you do that?

BRIK. How could I not do it? You are a great poet. I write articles on the uses of trochaic tetrameter with dactylic endings. I have argued in print that art is nothing but vanity. I even had you believing it. But the truth is, I have worshipped you like a god. Your poems are like holy mysteries to me.

MAYAKOVSKY. I'm not a poet any more. I'm a manufacturer of bullshit for the state. You've made me into that.

BRIK. Whatever you are, you've made yourself into it. And lately you've committed some serious errors in judgement which are increasingly troubling to us. You've even betrayed the woman you've been betraying me with. You've taken up with a white Russian whore in Paris. You nearly married her before she dumped you for a French Viscount. This is very disappointing. And deeply insulting to my wife.

MAYAKOVSKY. Insulting to your wife?

BRIK. And you have persistently refused to join the party.

MAYAKOVSKY. I don't want to be a member of any party. I've acquired habits which are not easily reconciled with organized activity.

BRIK. This is exactly the problem. That sort of behavior has consequences. And sooner or later, consequences come to get you.

(The **FIRST** *and* **SECOND SKELETON CLOWNS** *appear, looking downstage towards* **MAYAKOVSKY**.*)*

MAYAKOVSKY. What about Lily? Has she been spying on me, too?

BRIK. Lily does whatever she pleases.

MAYAKOVSKY. God.

BRIK. God has nothing to do with it.

MAYAKOVSKY. Last night I dreamed I went to the funeral of a ventriloquist's dummy. I looked into the coffin and saw my own face.

(Pause.)

So what do you want me to do? Shoot myself in the head?

BRIK. It's not my place to tell you what to do. Although I've heard it said that the heart is better. But of course, you have no gun.

MAYAKOVSKY. I have a gun.

BRIK. But you have no bullets.

MAYAKOVSKY. I have one bullet.

(Pause.)

Are you here?

BRIK. Am I here? Where else would I be?

MAYAKOVSKY. Am I imagining you? Are you really here?

BRIK. No. I'm somewhere else entirely. I'm in Berlin, with Lily. I'm pleasuring her on a bed of roses with the tongue of an aardvark.

MAYAKOVSKY. Then where am I?

BRIK. Nowhere. You are nowhere.

(Pause.)

MAYAKOVSKY. Look over there in the shadows. Do you see him? It's the poet Mayakovsky. You can just make him out in the dark, broken mirror. Let us stop this insane comedy. If they light up the stars, that means somebody needs them, doesn't it? It means someone wants them there. Tell Satan when he leaves to turn the stars off.

> (**MAYAKOVSKY** *finishes his drink and begins moving upstage, the* **FIRST** *and* **SECOND SKELETON CLOWNS** *on either side of him, and sings, to the tune of* **"THE INTERNATIONALE"***:)*

WE HAVE FOUGHT
TO FREE MANKIND FROM TSARS,
AND NOW WE'RE BEHIND BARS.
THE ROYALS ARE DEAD.
WHO'LL SAVE US
FROM THE REDS?

> (**MAYAKOVSKY** *disappears into the shadows with the Clowns.*)

BRIK. A funny thing happened to my dearest friend, a man I loved very deeply, the poet Mayakovsky. He shot himself in the heart.

> (*Sound of a loud gunshot, off. The* **THIRD SKELETON CLOWN** *enters with a folded piece of paper, gives it to* **BRIK**, *goes out.* **BRIK** *unfolds the paper and reads.*)

By order of Comrade Stalin, Vladimir Mayakovsky is officially designated a genius and the great poet of the revolution and of the Soviet state. Any indifference to his memory is considered an act of treason. To speak ill of his work is a crime punishable by death.

> (*Folds up the paper.*)

I know my dear friend Mayakovsky would have been very pleased.

19.
The Intercourse Of Animals

LYUBOV. You've been waiting for me again. You're there every night, when I come out of the theatre. I don't need you to walk me home.

BELY. It's dangerous to walk alone.

LYUBOV. The theatre has always been dangerous. During the revolution they were shooting people dead in the lobby. It's just the risk one takes.

BELY. Why do you still do this? It's so difficult, and there's so little money in it.

LYUBOV. Meyerhold says I'm a good actress. He says I've grown a lot since Blok died. He says I'm braver now.

BELY. Brik told me Meyerhold is under investigation. What if they send him to the labor camps? What will happen to his theatre then? What will happen to you? To remove the director is like the death of God. The universe will drift into chaos, and all of you will be lost.

LYUBOV. I'm tired. I need to go home now.

BELY. Why do you avoid me?

LYUBOV. I don't know what to say to you.

BELY. Are you afraid to be alone with me?

LYUBOV. I don't want to give you false hope.

BELY. False hope? Do you think I have any hope?

LYUBOV. Then what are you doing here?

BELY. Sometimes I put on a mask and sit in my room for days thinking of you. I put on the mask because I have no face. I was going to jump off a bridge but I was afraid I'd land on a fishing boat and I didn't want to break my ankles. I don't know what I'm saying. I don't know what I'm doing. I feel like an old woman rummaging in a tub full of boiled crabs. Did you know that I have considered murdering you and then killing myself? No. It's all right. I was joking. When you told me you loved me, you were joking. I'm joking. You're joking. We're

all joking. We're all clowns. It's Meyerhold's dream.
You did love me once. Does that mean nothing to you?

LYUBOV. You can believe what you like, but it won't change
anything. Please let me go now.

BELY. Tell me you never loved me.

LYUBOV. Why do you torture me like this? You torture me
and torture yourself and all for nothing. What's the
point? It all happened such a long time ago.

BELY. Tell me you never loved me, and I'll go away and
never bother you again.

LYUBOV. I never loved you. I didn't love you then, I haven't
loved you since then, I don't love you now, and I will
never love you. I will never love you. I will never love
you.

BELY. Not today, but maybe tomorrow.

LYUBOV. No, not tomorrow. Never. I have never loved
you and I don't love you now and I will never, never,
never, never love you. Now I must go and feed the
dog or bury the dog or learn my lines or something.
It's quite exciting, acting for Meyerhold. You're either
on a trapeze or standing on your head. It keeps me
from thinking. That's what art is for. Art is what you do
instead of living. Or dying. I forget which.

BELY. Is it not possible for you to love anyone?

LYUBOV. No. I could love any number of people. Just not
you.

BELY. Why? Why not me?

LYUBOV. Because you are the one who loves me.

> (**LYUBOV** *turns her back on him, walks up into the*
> *shadows and disappears. She will not return.*)

BELY. Because I am the one who loves her. She'd rather love
a dead man who slept with whores and died of syphilis.
Yes. Well. They are publishing my memoirs soon. I shall
be as kind to the both of you as you deserve.

MANDELSTAM. (*To* **ANNA,** *as* **BELY** *puts on his coat and finishes*
his drink.) Do you know how Bely died? He finally got

permission to publish his memoirs. He waited forever
for his author's copies. Finally, the box arrived. He tore
the package open in great excitement and discovered
they'd inserted an introduction which said that all of
Bely's writing was nothing but outmoded and worthless
hackwork.

BELY. Here betrayal. There illusions. Caught in the spider's
web. A woman is an abyss one falls into, like a poem.
To become entangled in one's constructs is to go mad.
The nights pass, one after the other, in quiet madness.
There is no mercy in art. There is no mercy in love.
There is no mercy. The secret behind everything is that
nothing means anything.

> (**BELY** *puts on his hat and moves upstage, where*
> *the* **SECOND SKELETON CLOWN** *is waiting for*
> *him.*)

MANDELSTAM. Bely put on his hat, walked to the nearest
book store, bought up all the copies of his memoirs,
ripped out the introductions, and put them back on
the shelves. Then he went to the next bookstore. He
was ripping out these introductions when he had a
stroke and dropped dead.

> (**BELY** *disappears into the shadows, arm in arm*
> *with the* **SECOND SKELETON CLOWN**.)

One by one they kill us, until nobody is left with a
brain. History is a game of catastrophes, and we are the
billiard balls. Somebody else has got the stick. At night,
the wolves come into the city.

BRIK. We learn from the Kama Sutra that the intercourse of
animals, as far as we know, is not preceded by thoughts
of any kind.

20.
I Have These Questions For The Moon

MANDELSTAM. I wake up in the middle of the night, absolutely certain Akhmatova has been arrested. It's the same way poems come to me. If I knew how they came, they wouldn't come. In my mind's eye, I have seen a corpse in the ravine. I must go out to the ravine to look for Akhmatova's corpse in the rain. But my wife talks me into coming back to bed.

ANNA. I like your wife very much. I can't imagine how she puts up with you.

MANDELSTAM. Yes. Nadezhda is tough. She says my jokes are going to get me killed. But I'll go mad if I stop making jokes. When I stop making jokes, that will be the day they've destroyed me utterly. Don't act like a clown, she says. But I am not the clown here.

(The **THIRD SKELETON CLOWN** *appears, looks down stage at Mandelstam.)*

They'll drive us all mad. Khlebnikov carried his manuscripts around Petersburg in a pillowcase, following the birds, and starved to death. I have made things strange by making them impossibly complicated. But Stalin makes everything simple. There is life. There is death. There is death in life. There is life in death. The system selects for stupidity and mediocrity. It weeds out the truth tellers, drives them mad and kills them. My brain is a bag of dead hornets. Death crawling towards me like a spider.

(The **FIRST SKELETON CLOWN** *appears, looks at* **MANDELSTAM.***)*

You take one streetcar. I'll take the other one. We'll see who dies first. Burn all your manuscripts but save what you scribbled in the margins. God is lurking in the marginalia. And save what you write in your dreams. I have studied the science of goodbyes. All the elegant mirage of Petersburg was a dream. Crawling up hill

on our knees to Stalin. Painting birds on the walls in
blood. The blood on the walls has not yet dried.

(*The* **SECOND SKELETON CLOWN** *appears, looks
at* **MANDELSTAM**.)

All right, so I wrote a little poem about how Stalin was a
homicidal maniac with fat fingers like grub worms and
a mustache like a cockroach, and I happened to read
it to a few friends. So he can't take a joke? Who knew?

(*The* **FIRST**, **SECOND** *and* **THIRD SKELETON
CLOWNS** *begin to converge on* **MANDELSTAM**.)

I open my mouth to cry for help but nothing comes
out. But you don't have to understand a poem to love
it. It's the same with people.

ANNA. I was there when they came in the night to take
Mandelstam away. They threw his manuscripts on the
floor and walked all over them with their filthy boots.

(*The* **FIRST SKELETON CLOWN** *stops at*
MANDELSTAM*'s right.*)

Prison, then exile, then prison, then exile, then
madness, then death. What was his crime? This poem
or that poem?

(*The* **SECOND SKELETON CLOWN** *stops at*
MANDELSTAM*'s left.*)

No. For nothing. We are taken away and killed for
nothing. The same nothing that lives in Nevsky
Prospect in the middle of the night when nobody is
there. The nothing that lurks in my empty rooms when
I come home in the dark. The nothing that waits on the
staircase landing. The Devil flickering in the gaslight. I
have these questions for the moon.

(*The* **THIRD SKELETON CLOWN** *stops just upstage
of* **MANDELSTAM**.)

MANDELSTAM. Kellipot is the tree of death. Chaos. Disorder.
The shells or husks that surround the Tree of life, like
the layers of an onion. In this place, the Devil lights the

lamps so everything will look like what it's not. Until you no longer feel humiliation from things done to you, you are not ready. This is no joke.

> (*The* **THIRD SKELETON CLOWN** *takes* **MANDELSTAM** *by the shoulders, the* **FIRST** *and* **SECOND SKELETON CLOWNS** *by his arms, and they take him upstage. He stops for a moment, turns back to* **ANNA**.)

Oh, wait. I didn't tell you. I met God at the circus. He was cleaning up after the elephants. I told him, you shouldn't be doing this. You're God, you should be sitting on a throne in Heaven. And God looked at me, and he said, What, and give up show business?

> (*The* **SKELETON CLOWNS** *take* **MANDELSTAM** *upstage and he disappears into the shadows.*)

21.
Why Do You Have Clowns?

STANISLAVSKY. *(A voice from the shadows.)* Meyerhold? Can't anybody here tell me where Meyerhold lives?

MEYERHOLD. Stanislavsky? What are you doing here?

STANISLAVSKY. I've been wandering around and around the block like Moses in the Wilderness. When I ask people where you live, they scuttle away like roaches.

MEYERHOLD. You don't look well. Sit down.

STANISLAVSKY. No. If I sit down, I'll probably never get up again.

MEYERHOLD. Nobody comes here now. Only Pasternak and Eisenstein were brave enough to come. It's like I've got the plague. They've taken my theatre away from me. And nobody will hire us. Zinaida hasn't eaten. I haven't eaten. Stalin has decided my productions are counter revolutionary. It's dangerous to be seen with me.

STANISLAVSKY. What are they going to do to me? I'll be dead soon anyway. I want you to come and help me run my theater.

MEYERHOLD. But why would you want me there? You're against everything I've been doing.

STANISLAVSKY. Theatrical fashion comes and goes. You find a truth. Over time it starts to look like a lie. Someone else comes in and turns everything upside down. Then what they do starts looking like a lie and somebody else turns them upside down. This is the natural ebb and flow of art. The important thing is that the investigation continues. I admit, I'm bewildered by some of the things you do. But your mind is alive. Your soul is engaged. You are making your own investigations into truth. I'd rather give my theatre to you than to an army of boot licking disciples. Come and work with me. Then I'll know that when I'm dead, my theatre will at least not be left in the hands of a bunch of sycophantic mediocrities who take everything I say as gospel and turn it into lies.

MEYERHOLD. They could destroy your theatre.

STANISLAVSKY. You kill one theatre, another one pops up around the corner. That's why the fuckers are so terrified of us. I'll expect you at the theatre first thing in the morning.

MEYERHOLD. Thank you.

STANISLAVSKY. There is much good work to be done still. We'll figure it out together and let our grandchildren decide we were both full of shit.

> (**STANISLAVSKY** *turns and walks away upstage, escorted by the* **FOURTH** *and* **FIFTH SKELETON CLOWNS***, and disappears into the shadows.*)

MEYERHOLD. I'll have a theatre again. There's still a chance. There's still hope.

> (*The* **FIRST** *and* **SECOND SKELETON CLOWNS** *appear. They grab* **MEYERHOLD** *and drag him to a table up left.*)

Wait. What are you doing? Stop it. I haven't done anything. I'm going to take over Stanislavsky's theatre.

> (*The* **THIRD SKELETON CLOWN** *turns a table over. The* **FIRST** *and* **SECOND SKELETON CLOWNS** *throw* **MEYERHOLD** *down behind it, where we can't see him. The* **FOURTH** *and* **FIFTH SKELETON CLOWNS** *appear and start beating him with canes.*)

Ahhhhhhhhh.   AHHHHHHHHHHHHH.
AHHHHHHHHHHHHH.

> (*The stage has been gradually getting darker.* **BRIK** *appears and goes to sit at his own table down right, in a little circle of light, as the* **CLOWNS** *continue to beat* **MEYERHOLD** *savagely across the stage behind the table.*)

BRIK. They were torturing someone today. I found it quite exciting. I felt as if I could almost see the face God wears when he takes off his mask. There is a certain sense of power one gets, being a critic. The power to extend mercy or to destroy. This feeling I had, watching the torture, was like that, but much more intense. I found I was almost sexually aroused. I remember looking at my fingernails and thinking, look at that. It's true. Your fingernails continue to grow after you're dead. Then I noticed the person they were torturing seemed familiar. Who is that? I asked. Some theatrical scum, they said. The son of a bitch directs plays. Then I realized it was my friend Meyerhold. He was made to lie face down and beaten on the soles of his feet and spine until his legs were covered with internal hemorrhaging. He howled and wept as if boiling water was being poured on him. It was really quite theatrical.

> *(The* **FIRST SKELETON CLOWN** *carries a wooden chair to center stage and sets it down with a bang. The* **SECOND** *and* **FOURTH SKELETON CLOWNS** *drag* **MEYERHOLD** *to center stage and sit him in the chair. He is now in a circle of light, surrounded by darkness, the only other light being that over* **BRIK** *'s table in the downstage corner.)*

MEYERHOLD. Why are you doing this to me? I don't know anything. I haven't done anything. I direct plays. I just direct plays.

BRIK. What is your name?

MEYERHOLD. You know my name.

> *(The* **THIRD SKELETON CLOWN** *touches* **MEYERHOLD** *on the neck with his cane, using it like a cattle prod. A loud buzzing sound, like electricity.* **MEYERHOLD** *jerks and screams.)*

AHHHHHHHHHHHH.

BRIK. Please just answer the questions. What is your name?

MEYERHOLD. Vsevolod Meyerhold.

BRIK. What is your occupation?

MEYERHOLD. I've just told you my occupation.

> (*The* **SECOND SKELETON CLOWN** *touches* **MEYERHOLD** *on the neck with the cane. The same loud electric buzzing, and same reaction.*)

AHHHHHHHHHHHHHH. I'm a theatrical director.

BRIK. Wife's name?

MEYERHOLD. Zinaida Raikh. She's an actress in my company.

BRIK. So you believe your wife is living?

MEYERHOLD. As far as I know. Why do you say that?

BRIK. So you're not aware that your wife is dead?

MEYERHOLD. My wife is dead?

BRIK. A very mysterious incident. Apparently two unknown persons broke into your apartment and stabbed her repeatedly in her back, chest and face. You'll need to replace the carpet.

MEYERHOLD. You've murdered my wife? You despicable, cowardly vermin have murdered my wife?

> (*The* **FIRST SKELETON CLOWN** *touches* **MEYERHOLD**'s *neck with his cane.*)

AHHHHHHHHHHH.

> (*The* **FIFTH SKELETON CLOWN** *touches* **MEYERHOLD**'s *ear with his cane.*)

AHHHHHHHHHHHHHHHHHHH.

BRIK. But there is good news. Your apartment was given to relatives of Comrade Beria.

MEYERHOLD. Zinaida never hurt anyone in her life. She's the best person I ever knew.

BRIK. Despite the fact that after her marriage to you, she continued to have sexual relations with her first husband, the poet Yesenin?

MEYERHOLD. That's a filthy lie.

(The **FOURTH SKELETON CLOWN** *touches* **MEYERHOLD**'s *left nipple with the cane.)*

AHHHHHHHHHHHHH.

(The **FIRST SKELETON CLOWN** *touches* **MEYERHOLD**'s *right nipple with the cane.)*

AHHHHHHHHHHHHHHHH.

BRIK. We have photographs, if you'd like to see them. Your wife was quite beautiful, especially when she was naked. She appears to have been a very enthusiastic sexual partner. You will be pleased to hear that this extramarital activity ceased once Yesenin hung himself. Now tell me, why have you engaged in counterrevolutionary activity?

MEYERHOLD. I have never engaged in counterrevolutionary activity. I direct plays.

BRIK. Would you consider your plays to be effective propaganda?

MEYERHOLD. I don't direct propaganda. I direct plays.

(The **SECOND SKELETON CLOWN** *touches* **MEYERHOLD**'s *testicles with the cane. Even bigger jolt of electricity and buzz.)*

AHHHHHHHHHHHHHHHHH.

BRIK. Why do you have clowns in your plays?

MEYERHOLD. I don't know. I like clowns.

BRIK. Are you making fun of the Soviet government?

MEYERHOLD. Why are you doing this to me? I've never done anything to hurt you or anybody else.

BRIK. People like you hurt us just by existing. And yet, we are inclined to have mercy on this occasion.

(Pause.)

No. I don't think so. Take him out and kill him.

(The **THIRD** *and* **FOURTH SKELETON CLOWNS** *drag* **MEYERHOLD** *off the chair and towards the upstage darkness.)*

MEYERHOLD. *(Screaming as they drag him.)* Criminals. Maniacs. Monsters.

> *(He disappears into the darkness.)*

BRIK. Very good. Honest human emotion. The thing you artistic types never seem to understand is that—

> *(Sound of a gunshot off, loud.)*

Next.

22.

Dangerous To Write

(The **FIRST** *and* **FIFTH SKELETON CLOWNS** *take* **ANNA** *to center stage and sit her in the chair. She is now in a pool of light, surrounded by darkness. Then they retreat upstage to watch from the darkness with the other three* **SKELETON CLOWNS.***)*

BRIK. *(Still from his circle of light down right.)* Name?

ANNA. Anna Akhmatova.

BRIK. Occupation?

ANNA. Poet.

BRIK. But what is your actual occupation?

ANNA. Poet. I'm a poet.

BRIK. This is how you support yourself?

ANNA. This is how I live.

BRIK. Marital status?

ANNA. Widow. With one son. Do you have my son? What have you done with my son?

BRIK. How many men have you had sexual relations with?

ANNA. Hundreds. Thousands. The entire population of Uzbekistan. Seven or eight. I don't know. Why would you ask me a question like that? Let my son go and I'll tell you anything you want to know. I'll write poems about how wonderful Stalin's mustache is. Just let my child alone.

BRIK. How many men have you loved?

ANNA. It depends on what you think love is. Just one, perhaps, but I keep changing my mind about which one it is. He keeps changing his masks. There was the one who deflowered me, the one who loved me until he had me, the one who painted me in the nude, and one who did mosaics, the Babylonian, the musician, the art critic—what a prize he turned out to be.

BRIK. The one in whose apartment you lived and fornicated for years while his wife was also in residence?

ANNA. If you know, then why did you ask?

BRIK. How many men have killed themselves over you?

ANNA. I don't know. What time is it now?

BRIK. But who did you love? Who did you actually love?

ANNA. Perhaps none of them. Perhaps I have never loved a man. I have suffered much, and I have made them suffer over me, but perhaps I never really loved any of them. The purpose of men is to suffer for you and to make you suffer so you can write poems.

BRIK. And what is the purpose of poems? Why do you write them?

ANNA. Why do you breathe?

BRIK. In order to live.

ANNA. There you go.

BRIK. Why didn't you leave Russia when you had the chance?

ANNA. I don't know. Why didn't you?

BRIK. How many of your lovers did you betray?

ANNA. They betrayed me. Everybody betrays everybody. It's the nature of love. Are all your interrogations as bizarre as this?

BRIK. Then you admit you've committed acts of betrayal?

ANNA. Why do you need to know this? Do you get so little satisfaction from your own lives that you'd rather poke around in mine instead? What have you done with my son?

BRIK. It's rather late in the day for you to be worried about that, now, isn't it? You were too busy being a poet and taking lovers to worry about him when he needed you. Now it's too late.

ANNA. Your voice is familiar. Do I know you?

BRIK. Nobody knows me. I'm a critic.

ANNA. So there is no hope.

BRIK. There never was.

ANNA. Has your wife betrayed you? Is that why you're so interested in these matters?

BRIK. It is very dangerous to talk back to us.

ANNA. It's dangerous to write, especially poetry, where you listen and put down what your subconscious gives you, even if you don't understand it. It's like walking in your sleep. You think my poems are about me, but the minute one starts writing the poem, the poem starts writing you, and you become a fictional personage.

BRIK. So in other words you've spent your entire life constructing evasions and lies.

ANNA. Except that in the attempt to conceal one thing, you reveal something deeper and more strange. A poem is an abyss. The longer you stare into the darkness, the better you can see, but much is still hidden, and you never get to the bottom. And in everything you write there are omens of the future, especially in the oddest images, that don't seem to make sense. As you write you can feel the future ripening into the past. The unreality of the masquerade. Writing is a kind of magic spell. You write it, and then it happens to you.

BRIK. You people make me sick. You all think you're so important, just because you create things and we can't, but in fact, the author is nobody. If Pushkin hadn't written *Eugene Onegin* somebody else would have. All authors are expendable. All that remains is the written artifact. Who cares who created it, or who he slept with?

ANNA. Apparently you do. I know who you are.

BRIK. You have no idea who I am.

ANNA. You're a man whose wife's lover shot himself in the chest, and when he was dead, she broke her word and divorced you, and married somebody else. And you've been helping them torture and murder people ever since. That's who you are. What a foolish thing, to die for love. Olga made it into a puppet show. But to die for love is not a thing that should be mocked.

We have been childish and selfish and that poor stupid boy is dead and perhaps all this subsequent butchery and horror is not entirely unrelated to that capacity for betrayal that is blind to consequences to ourselves or other people. But God preserves everything. He keeps it all in his attic. There are many birdcages, and trunks full of wedding pictures and candlesticks. And in one old trunk he keeps the corpse of his beloved. You were some sort of a writer once, weren't you? he said. And tore up my identity papers. But I'm not afraid of you. When I was young I wasn't afraid of anything, and I'm still not afraid of the cockroaches who plant their bugs in my umbrella stand and spy on me. But sometimes in the middle of Nevsky Prospect late at night when nobody is there and it's very still, I am terrified to cross the street. I look in all directions and see nothing, and that is the terrifying thing. To be in the middle of a big, empty street is like falling between the stars. And when I come home at night and put the key in the lock and open the door I think something is waiting for me in those empty rooms. I am afraid of stairways and landings, I come to them and I can't move. Let me make it easy for you. The answer to your question is, yes. I have committed treason. I have betrayed all those I loved by writing about them. And I will continue doing this until I die. So I suppose you had better just take me out and shoot me in the head like everybody else.

BRIK. It would be quite easy for me to do that. Life or death. Like flipping a coin. But it has been decided that you will not be killed today. I don't know why. Perhaps we'll kill you tomorrow. Or perhaps we'll let you live, and watch your child suffer instead. Go on. Get out. Go home and write more poems that nobody will read.

ANNA. I'm afraid to go home. There's a dead man on the staircase.

BRIK. Then write a poem about it. Or just step over him and move on. In the end, it's much the same. I have the same nightmare every night. I am climbing a staircase with rose pattern wall paper. I feel a clutching at my heart. Could it be love? I think. No. Fortunately, it is just a fatal heart attack. Which is, on the whole, I suspect, a much less painful experience than loving a mortal creature.

(Sound of the wind. **BRIK** *walks up into the darkness to where the five* **SKELETON CLOWNS** *are waiting for him.)*

Hello, comrades. What's kept you so long?

(The **SKELETON CLOWNS** *take him rudely and grotesquely by the elbows, feet and head and carry him face down off into the darkness. Sound of the wind.)*

ANNA. And I only am left alone to tell the tale. A poet and a swarm of ghosts. But how can one sing in the midst of this horror? All of that wondrous strangeness vanished now. Meyerhold shot. Mandelstam insane and dead in a prison camp. Tsvetayeva hanged herself. Loneliness envelopes everything like poison mist. It's better not to think about what's lurking behind the mirrors. In order to survive in this place, one requires a sense of the ridiculous. Somebody is always listening. Somebody is always watching. Tea with raspberry jam and arsenic, on the edge of the wine-dark sea, red with the blood of poets. When we have tea there is no sugar. Or we have sugar but the tea's run out. I can't sleep, but I can write. I can't eat, but I can write. No matter what indignities they put me through, I can scribble on the inside of my coffin lid. But what's the point? Passing by the butcher shop, a pile of decapitated heads. They have killed everybody I loved. Why have they left me alive? I give you my reflection in the water. Remember the one who loved you. There is nothing else.

(Sound of the Couperin, as at the beginning, and in the shadows around her we can make out

TAMARA, *who's been hiding behind a table in the shadows, watching.)*

TAMARA. Anna. Come and dance.

ANNA. I don't dance.

TAMARA. Come and dance, Anna.

ANNA. Foolish girl. Don't you know that everybody here is dead? What's the point?

TAMARA. *(Comes over to* ANNA, *takes her hand.)* There is no point. There is only the dance. And the dance is very beautiful.

> *(*TAMARA *begins to dance, inviting* ANNA *to mirror her.* ANNA *watches, hesitates, and then, sadly, she begins to dance. She and* TAMARA *dance.* TAMARA *gradually fades into the shadows and disappears, and* ANNA, *now caught up in it, dances all alone. Then, sound of a door opening, off, and some early morning light streams down the steps. The music fades, but* ANNA *continues to dance.)*

TOMASHEVSKY. *(A voice from up the staircase.)* Anna? Are you still here?

ANNA. *(Stops dancing, reluctantly, looking up into the light.)* I don't know.

TOMASHEVSKY. *(Coming down the steps.)* Thank God you're all right. I've had a terrible time. I got to the doctor's and it wasn't there any more. The whole block was a huge pile of rubble. And then I was accosted by a ridiculous gang of hooligans who demanded to see my papers, and it's taken me most of the night to convince them I'm who I am. Are you all right?

ANNA. Yes.

TOMASHEVSKY. Is your mind clearing?

ANNA. Yes.

TOMASHEVSKY. Have you been here alone all this time?

ANNA. No. Somebody was here. But they're all gone now. I'm the only one left.

TOMASHEVSKY. Well, come with me. It's just dawn. We'll get you home.

ANNA. I am home.

> *(As* **TOMASHEVSKY** *helps her up the steps and lights begin to fade, we can hear the others singing from somewhere off.)*

ALL BUT ANNA AND TOMASHEVSKY.

COME TO ME,
MY LITTLE RUSSIAN SWEETHEART,
LET ME HOLD YOU
NOW BEFORE THE DAWN.
SOON ENOUGH
WE WILL BOTH BE FORGOTTEN,
TIME WILL STOP—
AND THEN IT WILL MOVE ON.
SOON ENOUGH
WE WILL ALL BE FORGOTTEN.
TIME WILL STOP—
AND WE WILL ALL BE GONE.

> *(Darkness.)*

NOTEBOOK: NIGHTS AT THE STRAY DOG CAFÉ

In September 1941, during the siege of Leningrad (now once again St Petersburg), poet Anna Akhmatova and literary historian Boris Tomashevsky were caught in a bombing raid, and took shelter in a cellar that they soon realized was once, many years earlier, the Stray Dog Café.

The Stray Dog was located in a former wine cellar at the corner of Italyanskaya Street, on Mikhailovskaya Square in Petersburg. Owned by an actor, Boris Pronin, it was, in the second decade of the twentieth century, the vibrant center of bohemian Russian artistic life. It opened after the theatres closed, a half hour before midnight. You went down a narrow stone staircase and through a doorway so low that it would knock your hat off. When you entered the Stray Dog, you had to sign a big book covered in pig skin. Writers and artists got in free. For others, there was a small cover charge. The windows were blocked to keep the rest of the world out. Flowers, birds and commedia characters were painted on the walls and curved ceilings by Olga Sudeikina's husband Sergey. At one or two in the morning things would be going full blast, music, dancing, plays, puppet shows, poetry recitals, much good natured heckling and yelling back and forth. By three it would start to gradually clear out, as couples paired off, but it stayed open until dawn.

In March 1915 the Stray Dog was closed due to wartime censorship. On October 25 the Comedian's Halt opened in another cellar, and many of the old regulars showed up there. In 1917, during the Revolution, the Stray Dog was opened again as the Comedians' Shelter.

At the Stray Dog, the first joyous fruits of social rebellion, the casting off of convention, ushered in an extraordinary period of intense and astonishing creativity. On any given night you might see the poets Akhmatova, Tsvetayeva, Pasternak or Mandelstam, the dancers Karsavina and Sudeikina, the choreographer Fokine, the poet and playwright Mayakovsky, the director Meyerhold, the critic Brik, his beautiful wife Lily, the poet and novelist Bely, or just about anybody in the artistic world of early twentieth century Russia.

But towards the end of her life, Akhmatova began to ask herself if there might be some connection between the infidelities and betrayals of the Stray Dog and the nightmare the revolution turned into. It's not that she imagined that who slept with who in 1912 had somehow created Stalin. It's that the joyously obsessive self-gratification evident in the artists of her generation, a reaction to the repressive society they were born into, carried within it the seeds of its own destruction, and theirs. That in rejecting the repressive values of the old society, they had left behind some other values that were worth preserving, like compassion and loyalty, something which the coming horrors of the Stalinist era would teach them again before it killed them. This is the legacy of repressive societies: the generation which is finally in a position to rebel against repression throws out the baby with the bath water. In their joy at exercising their newly found freedom, they abandon values necessary for decent human relations. Revolutions tend not to stop until they've gone too far. They don't know where too far is until they get there, and then it's too late. A good thing to depose the Tsar? Yes. But is it also a good thing to take his children into the basement and shoot them in the head? A good thing to have sexual freedom? Yes. A good thing to betray and abandon those who love you? Mandelstam tries to convince Mayakovsky that there are some values in the old civilization worth keeping. But Mayakovsky won't have it. From his point of view, that is just making one's self a flunky to the old oppressive powers. For Mayakovsky, everything must be destroyed. Everything must be made new. And the last thing he destroys is himself.

Years later, Camus would argue for the retaining of some basic humanistic values and a sense of perspective, and was bitterly attacked for it by his friend Sartre, who defended Stalin and called Camus a traitor to the cause. These patterns repeat themselves in human experience. Repression. Rebellion against repression, first a good thing, goes too far, and begins to behave repressively itself. A reasonable person who tries to point this out gets his head chopped off. The good guys defeat the bad guys, begin to define themselves as always and forever the good guys, and slowly turn into the bad guys. People are not fond of subtle distinctions. They're not comfortable with irony. They want simple answers. The attempt to understand the other side of the question is considered weakness. If God is on our side, then we can do anything, including taking our oppressor's daughters into the basement and shooting them in the head. It is that poison of selfish intolerance and indifference to suffering that Akhmatova sees reflected in the Stalinist nightmare she was to live through later.

A snowflake on my hand. A masquerade. An apparition. Why does the wine burn like poison? I am a ghost in the doorway. I hope you haven't dared to bring the Prince of Darkness here. Salome's dance. The future ripens in the past. The past rots in the future. This is the festival of dead leaves. You will stop laughing before dawn.

The world appears, says Heisenberg, as a complicated tissue of events in which connections of different kinds alternate or overlap or combine and thus determine the texture of the whole.

Associational thinking. Bergson and Coleridge. Image fragments. Incongruous juxtaposition creates unexpected meaning. Time as layers of consciousness, overlapping experience. A palimpsest. Past layers show through present experience, but also premonitions of the future. Past is linked by memory to the present which is linked by imagination to the future. Remembered images are symbols of emotional states, past, present and future, since imagination creates symbols of possible future emotional states.

Sometimes, as one writes, one stumbles upon images, apparently thrown up by chance in the churning of experience, which echo in one's head, and one writes them down, saves them, and they begin to coalesce mysteriously with other images, until some odd and totally unanticipated sense of significance appears, as if by magic, out of chaos. It is the subconscious that is doing the selecting of apparently random images from out of a vast number which bombard us daily. Those images which carry enough resonance to compel one to write them down acquire that resonance from their connection to things deep in our subconscious which have not yet risen to the surface.

Imagination is not just putting together fragments from the past in different combinations. It is also a kind of precognition, as in the dream state explored by J. W. Dunne in *An Experiment With Time*. There are many possible futures. Each imagined future is a different universe. To become violently attached to one possible future universe while being trapped in another is to go mad. Romantic love is just this sort of madness, as Rosalind points out in the Forest of Arden.

When one is in love, the world seems to be a forest of symbols, all suggesting the beloved. In fact, the subconscious is searching through the huge number of sensations and images we are presented with, looking for anything it can connect to the beloved. The beloved seems to be the key that unlocks the mystery of everything. The world is full of clues, all of them leading back to the beloved.

Collage. Palimpsest. The intersection of multi-dimensional labyrinths. As in Lacan, what we are is an assemblage of ever changing images. We look in the mirror and decide that is us. But it isn't us. It isn't anybody. It's just a reflection. We live in a labyrinth of desire lined with mirrors. I identify the other with myself. But the other is eternally the other. Desire is never fulfilled. One struggles to escape from love, and then, having escaped, feels only emptiness. The world is drained of meaning.

Max Ernst on multiple vision: It's a rainy day. Ernst finds himself in a village on the Rhine, looking at an illustrated catalogue of aids for various sorts of scientific demonstration, for anthropology, psychology, paleontology. The proximity of wildly dissociative images causes his brain to make a series of rapid and unusual connections, like memories of love or the illusions that come when one is half asleep. He finds himself cutting out and recombining these images, reproducing what he calls "that which saw itself in me," and creating images of his hallucination, transformed into dreams of his most secret desires.

In Akhmatova's poems, as in Proust, Joyce, Eliot, Bely, non-chronological order, apparently non-causal. The selection of specific detail. The connections arise from the personal associations the images suggest. Back and forth in time and space. Multiple exposure.

Dreamtime, for the native people of Australia, is the time of mythical ancestors. The places where paths cross are holy places. This is the dream labyrinth. Ayers Rock (Uluru) is not seen as a single spiritual object, but as the node of several different stories, all true. Creative power can flow through objects.

Associative methodology. Art lives, said the Formalist Eichenbaum, by interweaving and contrasting its own traditions, and refashioning them on principles of contrast, parody, shifting and sliding.

"The hardest thing of all," said Confucius, "is to find a black cat in a dark room. Especially if there is no cat."

Peter Hall's advice about doing Shakespeare: play on the line and keep going. McDuffy to John Rose: Look, doing Shakespeare is like being on a train. Stay on the train. Don't get off.

NIGHTS AT THE STRAY DOG CAFÉ

There was a young man named Mikhail Lindeberg who killed himself after Akhmatova rejected him. This might help explain her obsessive writing about Vsevolod Knyazev, who killed himself over Olga Sudeikina. Somehow these memories, and her feeling of not just sadness, but guilt, connect in her head with the date of Mandelstam's death in "Poem Without A Hero."

No matter how much you love, something always remains hidden. Arnold Bennett said: "And he now learnt that profound lesson that an individual must be taken or left in entirety, and that you cannot change an object merely because you love it."

The Russian Plays, a long cycle of plays tracing the history of Russia in the nineteenth and twentieth centuries, through the lives of its writers and others. Some of the plays are *Pushkin, Gogol, An Angler In The Lake Of Darkness, Emotion Memory, A Russian Play, Rasputin, Nights At The Stray Dog Café, Mandelstam, Marina.*

Some important characters in the Russian Plays:

Anna Akhmatova (1889–1966) Born Anna Andreyevna Gorenko near Odessa, in the Ukraine. Russian poet. Took the name Akhmatova from a Tatar ancestor. Married the poet Nikolay Gumilyov in 1910 after a long and troubled courtship. Her first book of poems was published in 1912. With Gumilyov and Osip Mandelstam, part of the Acmeist movement, in reaction to the mysticism of the Symbolists and the political rhetoric of the Bolsheviks. Married her second husband, the scholar of ancient history Vladimir Shileiko in 1918, left him for the art scholar Nikolai Punin in 1926. After 1922 it became increasingly difficult for her to get her work published. In 1946 she was condemned by the Central Committee and expelled from the Soviet writers' union, but after Stalin's death was eventually allowed to publish again. She appears in *Nights At The Stray Dog Café.*

Andrei Bely (1880–1934) Pen name of Boris Nikolayevich Bugayev. Poet, novelist, essayist. Born into a prominent family of intellectuals. His mother was a famous beauty, and the focus of a certain amount of scandalous speculation. Bely wrote novels, poems, philosophical essays and literary criticism, and was a champion of the Symbolist movement, great friend of the poet Blok, and deeply in love with Blok's wife Lyubov. His baroque, Joycean prose was much admired by Nabokov, who considered Bely's *Petersburg* to be one of the great novels of the twentieth century. He was also an early influence on the theatre of Meyerhold. His voluminous memoirs of Blok and others are compelling but unreliable. Later in life he was influenced by the anthroposophy of Rudolf Steiner. He appears in *Nights At The Stray Dog Café*.

Alexander Blok (1880–1921) Russian Symbolist poet. Son of aristocratic parents, married Lyubov Mendeleev, daughter of the creator of the periodic table of the elements, in 1903. Published his first book of poems in 1904. Meyerhold directed his play, *The Puppet Show*, at Vera Komissarzhevskaya's theatre in St. Petersburg in 1906. By the time of the Revolution he was the most famous poet in Russia. A central figure in the Symbolist movement, he turned away from his earlier mysticism and supported the Revolution, but ultimately was horrified at its excesses. Worshipped his beautiful actress wife but slept with others instead and died of what was perhaps venereal disease. He appears in *Nights At The Stray Dog Café*.

Lyubov Blok (1881–1939) Wife of the poet Blok, daughter of Mendeleev, who invented the periodic table of the elements. Famously beautiful, Blok and Bely saw her as the embodiment of the World Soul, and Bely was obsessed with her. She eventually became a successful actress, working with Meyerhold and others. She appears in *Nights At The Stray Dog Café*.

Lily Brik (1891–1978) Known as the muse of the Russian avant-garde. Born into a wealthy Jewish family in Moscow. Beautiful, intelligent and gifted, she was painted by Léger, Matisse and Chagall. She married Osip Brik in 1912. Her early ambition was to be the muse of a great poet; she married a critic. He suggested an open marriage, and insisted he was not bothered by her passionate affair with Vladimir Mayakovsky, who moved in with them. This affair continued from 1917 to 1923, but she remained very important in Mayakovsky's life until his suicide, for which some blamed her. She divorced Brik and in 1930 married a Soviet General who was executed in 1937 as part of Stalin's Moscow Trials. She continued championing Mayakovsky's work after his death, and even wrote a letter to Stalin complaining that it was being neglected. In 1938 she married another writer and lived with him until her suicide in 1978, when she was terminally ill. She wrote, sculpted, and made films. She was a close friend of Meyerhold, Pasternak and Picasso. She appears in *Nights At The Stray Dog Café*.

Osip Brik (1888–1945) Critic and avant-garde writer, formalist, futurist, husband of Mayakovsky's mistress, and member of the Cheka, the feared and despised secret police. Brik asserted famously that the author does not exist, only what is written, and that if Pushkin had never lived someone else would have written *Eugene Onegin* He was brilliant but not creative, was interested in photography and film, wrote screenplays, slept in the same room while his wife was copulating with Mayakovsky, and was present when others were tortured by the Cheka. Pasternak reports that he and other friends began to find Brik more and more repulsive as they realized how deeply he was involved in the Cheka's activities. In his youth he was obsessed with prostitutes and used to follow them around, watching them. Later, Stalin turned on him, and Brik joined the ranks of his former victims. Brik died of a heart attack while climbing stairs. He appears in *Nights At The Stray Dog Café*.

Anton Chekhov (1860–1904) One of the greatest of Russian writers, master of the short story and author some of the greatest Russian plays, including *The Seagull, Three Sisters, Uncle Vanya* and *The Cherry Orchard,* all produced by

Stanislavsky at the Moscow Art Theatre. He appears in *An Angler In The Lake Of Darkness* and *Emotion Memory*.

Fyodor Dostoyevsky (1821–1881) Russian novelist. Author of *Notes From Underground, The Double, The Gambler, Crime And Punishment, The Devils, The Idiot, The Brothers Karamazov.* He appears in *Dostoyevsky*.

Nikolay Gogol (1809–1852) Born in the Ukraine. Novelist, playwright, short story writer, friend of Pushkin. Master of the grotesque. Author of the stories "The Overcoat," "The Nose," "Diary of A Madman," the play *The Inspector General,* and the novel *Dead Souls.* He appears in *Pushkin* and *Gogol.*

Nikolay Gumilyov (1886–1921) Poet and adventurer. First husband of Akhmatova. With her and Mandelstam, the core of the Acmeist movement in poetry. An adventurer by nature, world traveler, excited by danger, compulsively unfaithful. Shot by the Secret Police in 1921. He appears in *Nights At The Stray Dog Café.*

Tamara Karsavina (1885–1978) Ballerina. Made her debut at the Marinsky Theatre in 1902, and stayed with that company until just after the Revolution. Created great roles in *The Firebird, Petrouchka, Pulcinella* and many other ballets. Danced with the Diaghilev Company. Worked with Stravinsky, Nijinsky, Fokine. Moved to London. She appears in *Nights At The Stray Dog Café.*

Velimir Khlebnikov (1885–1922) Russian poet. Extremely gifted but always strange. Son of an ornithologist, obsessed with birds. Studied math, Sanskrit, biology, Slavic studies. Numerology. Trying to find mathematical patterns in the past that would predict the future. A holy fool. Very poor. Insight and madness. Mathematical calculations predicting the end of the world. Starved to death. He appears in *Nights At The Stray Dog Café.*

Vsevolod Knyazev (d 1913) poet who shot himself on the staircase outside Olga Sudeikina's flat when she rejected him. In *Nights At The Stray Dog Café.*

Osip Mandelstam (1891–1938) After an early association with the Symbolist poets, Mandelstam helped start the Acmeist movement, in an attempt to avoid mysticism in favor of a more concrete approach, but in fact his work was very complex and in its own way rather mysterious. Increasingly disillusioned with the Revolution, he was first arrested in 1934, and again in 1938. His mind unhinged by exile and constant fear of rearrest, he died in a transit camp in December of 1938. His wife Nadezhda preserved his poems by memorizing them. He appears in *Nights At The Stray Dog Café* and *Mandelstam.*

Vladimir Mayakovsky (1893–1930) Russian poet and playwright. Joined the Bolsheviks at age 14, and began writing poems in prison. Organized street theatre, and met Meyerhold, who later directed his plays. Met Osip and Lily Brik in 1915, and lived with them mostly for the rest of his life, as Lily's lover and Osip's friend. Celebrated the Revolution, coming up with slogans for posters and such things, but found himself increasingly discouraged by the repressive nature of Soviet society. In despair over his love life and his work, he shot himself in the chest in 1930. Stalin declared him the greatest Soviet poet. He appears in *Nights At The Stray Dog Café.*

Vsevolod Meyerhold (1874–1940) Russian stage director. Worked with Stanislavsky, but broke with him later and rejected the psychological approach. Developed biomechanics, an approach to performance in which acting is seen as a mechanical process, actors functioning like cogs in a machine, and requiring great physical agility and skills. Inspired by the circus, the carnival, street performers. Ignored the rights of playwrights, declaring that the author should just write a kind of outline for him and then get out of the way. But his theatrical innovations were brave and often stunning. Originally an enthusiastic supporter of the Revolution, he was eventually arrested, tortured and shot by the Secret Police. He appears in *Nights At The Stray Dog Café.*

Boris Pasternak (1890–1960) Russian poet and author of the novel *Doctor Zhivago*. Did his best to get along with the Soviet government while helping his fellow writers as much as he could. Won the Nobel Prize in literature in 1958 but was forced to reject it. Stalin called him on the telephone to ask him what to do with Mandelstam. He appears in *Mandelstam*.

Aleksandr Pushkin (1799—837) greatly revered Russian poet, playwright, novelist and short story writer. Struggled with the Tsar's censors for much of his career. Killed by his wife's lover in a duel. Friend of Gogol. He appears in *Pushkin*.

Zinaida Raikh (1894–1939) Actress, married first to the poet Yesenin and later to the great experimental stage director Meyerhold, in many of whose productions she was prominent. Stabbed to death in her flat in 1939.

Grigory Rasputin (1869–1914) Russian mystic. Advisor to the Empress. Very difficult to kill. He appears in *Rasputin*.

Josef Stalin (1878–1953) Russian dictator and homicidal maniac. He appears in *Mandelstam*.

Konstantin Stanislavsky (1863–1938) Co-founder of the Moscow Art Theatre. Directed and acted in groundbreaking productions there of the plays of Chekhov. Developed a system of acting that focused on inner experience and memory, rejected by his pupil Meyerhold in favor of a more presentational, externally oriented and physical approach. The author of *An Actor Prepares, Building A Character, Creating A Role,* and *My Life In Art* He appears in *Emotion Memory* and *Nights At The Stray Dog Café*.

Olga glebova Sudeikina (1885 St Petersburg–1945 Paris) actress, dancer, painter, sculptor, translator, model. The Decadence Fairy. Imperial Theatre School 1905. Married Sergei Sudeikin 1907. Separated 1915. Classical and modern dance at the Maly and at cabarets. Autumn 1924 to Berlin, then Paris. Translator of French poetry, studied painting and sculpture. Loved and collected dolls and figurines, especially of Commedia figures, and puppets of all kinds. Left Russia with a suitcase full of porcelain dolls. In Paris, known as "the Lady With The Birds." Kept many birds in her small apartment, often uncaged. Many wrote poems to her. Did many performances at the Stray Dog. Short plays and scenes, danced, and lived with Akhmatova briefly after the Revolution. On New Year's Eve, the poet Vsevolod Knyazev, deeply in love with Olga, shot himself to death on the staircase outside her apartment when he discovered she was sleeping with someone else, perhaps Blok. For the rest of her life, Akhmatova felt guilty about this, although it's not entirely clear why, and wrote about it in her famous "Poem Without A Hero."

Leo Tolstoy (1828–1910) Russian novelist, short story writer, playwright, essayist and reformer, author of the novels *War and Peace, Resurrection, Anna Karenina*, the play *The Power of Darkness*, and the autobiographical trilogy *Childhood, Boyhood, Youth*. He appears in *An Angler In The Lake Of Darkness*.

Boris Tomashevsky (1890–1957) Russian formalist literary scholar and historian of Russian literature. Edited the first Soviet editions of Pushkin and Dostoyevsky. He appears in *Nights At The Stray Dog Café*.

Marina Tsvetayeva (1892–1941) poet, playwright and essayist. Passionate and brilliant. In despair over her life under Stalin, she hung herself in 1941. She appears in *Marina*.

Ivan Turgenev (1818–1883) novelist and playwright. Author of the novel *Fathers And Sons, A Sportsman's Sketches* and the great play, *A Month In The Country*. He appears in *An Angler In The Lake Of Darkness*.

Sergey Yesenin (1895–1925) Russian poet. Married first to Zinaida Raikh, then to Isadora Duncan. Wrote his suicide note in his own blood, then hung himself in 1925.

Blok, the Symbolist, in his youth, and his friend Bely, saw the world like Baudelaire did, as a forest of symbols. What we see is an illusion, it is maya. Behind it is another reality.

Poetry, by observing and investigating these symbols, is a way of getting at that deeper reality.

Mayakovsky, the Futurist, like his critic friend Brik, whose wife he shared, is a materialist. For him, reality is just what the world shows us. There is no secret, hidden reality. This is the world, and we must manipulate it to our benefit. The illusion is that any other world exists. All structures and systems of belief based on these "other reality" values are dangerous opiates and must be destroyed.

Mandelstam and the other Acmeists, Akhmatova and her first husband Gumilyov, take a more nuanced position. Like the Futurists, they reject the mysterious other world, the deeper reality of the Symbolists, and prefer to investigate the details of this one, the world we seem to perceive with our senses. But unlike the Futurists, Mandelstam is not hostile to the past, or to past literature. He wants to save and incorporate the best elements of the past as a means of discovering new ways of looking at and understanding reality, always with an eye towards the specific detail of experience as embodying value in itself.

Akhmatova is closer to Mandelstam, but while he tried to exclude himself from his poems, she makes herself and her emotions the center of them. For her, the emotion of the moment would seem to be, in the end, all that matters, both while it is happening and in retrospect, as in Pound's Pisan Cantos, where nothing matters but the quality of the affection that has carved the trace in the mind.

A symbol is picturing one thing in terms of another. It is a connection, a corridor in the labyrinth, a path in the forest of memory and experience. A symbol is always about memory, because you can't connect things you don't remember. And it's always about time, because there is no memory without time. And about emotion, because you don't bother to remember what you don't care about. A sign stands for one thing. A symbol is a pathway to a labyrinth of associated meanings.

The function of art, said the Formalists, is to make everything strange, so we can see it new. Somewhere, Kandinsky is eating imaginary bacon.

Art creates maps. Every play is a map of a partly imagined, partly remembered, partly unknown territory. We can only hope the audience is not killed by a charging rhino.

What we all dread most, said Chesterton, is a maze with no center.

The Russian Formalists believed that popular techniques rejuvenate high art, as in Dostoyevsky's recasting of the detective story in *Crime and Punishment* and *The Brothers Karamazov.* Meyerhold, reacting against Stanislavsky's attempt to base acting upon recalled emotion, preferred to work from external stimuli, in the manner of ancient strolling players and carnival folk. The thing I like best about Meyerhold is his obsession with getting the actors closer to the audience, and his brave and often brilliant investigation of different ways to tell a story. My own instincts bring me closer to Stanislavsky (and to Freud), in regard to approaching character, but I understand what Meyerhold is getting at, love his courage and some of his approaches to staging, and think some of his ideas are a useful antidote to the sort of emotional self-indulgence disciples of the Method can fall into.

My instincts continue to be eclectic. I'll use anything, any sort of convention, old, new, or bastard amalgam, if it feels right to tell the story. At different times, with different stories, different actors, different audiences and spaces, different approaches feel right. The point is to let the story you discover you are telling show you how it needs to manifest itself, and be open to what works. To become rigid about these matters is the death of creation in the soul. In Shakespeare and the Jacobeans, I find an expansive spirit that feels it can do anything on a stage, tell any story, use any convention (puppet show, dumb show, singing and dancing, dream and hallucination, spectacle, the mixture of tragedy and farce) but still ultimately care about the people as individuals, take great delight in the use of language to try and investigate their feelings and the apparent external reality, and in the psychology of human behavior. In more recent times, the work of Samuel Beckett, Harold Pinter, Peter Barnes, Tom Stoppard, and the early work of John Arden and Edward Bond show how various aspects of this Elizabethan/Jacobean tradition of storytelling can manifest themselves through a more contemporary lens. Meyerhold's work is fascinating and very exciting, and a necessary corrective to the self-indulgent worship of Stanislavsky, but in the end, any art that is afraid to see people as anything but objects and mechanisms is highly unsatisfying.

Meyerhold wanted to simplify acting and turn performance into a series of hieroglyphics, and to some extent, I wonder if he didn't succeed best, like Brecht, when he failed to conform to his own theories. That is, what results is most interesting to me when it seems to be the result of the confrontation of what Meyerhold and Brecht say they want with what they say they are trying to escape. In each case, the results transcend the theory, the way art transcends criticism. In their different ways, Meyerhold and Brecht were both running away not just from what they regarded as outmoded theatrical conventions but also from things inside them that terrified them. But the more we try to substitute technique or theory for the raw monstrosity of the human soul, the more the soul returns, if we are lucky, to subvert all our efforts.

For Meyerhold, the ensemble was everything. What happened on the stage was always a function of all the moving parts working together. No room for ego. Except perhaps for his own. For him, as for the Russian formalist critics, character was merely a function of plot, as in Propp's *Morphology of the Folktale*. For Stanislavsky, character was everything. All else flowed from that. Stanislavsky's work emerges from the tradition of the great Russian novelists, Tolstoy and Dostoyevsky, as does Chekhov's. Meyerhold is closer to older traditions, the folk tale, Commedia, the carnival.

Meyerhold was interested in deformation and estrangement rather than revelation of character. The contradictions of human behavior were what felt true to him. He didn't mind beginning with stock types, the sort of thing Stanislavsky abhorred, because if one first established a type, one then had something to subvert. I've often noticed, he said, that an actor blossoms out quite unexpectedly in a part when he's forced to subdue his natural characteristics.

The theatre needs to smell like coffee. There is an organ grinder playing "Kalinka" before the show. God looks after everything. He just does a terrible job. God plays the hurdy gurdy in the sewer.

Tamara dancing on a mirror, choreographed by Fokine, whose heart she has broken. Meyerhold called "mirror gazing" the actors ability to see himself from the side. How can I be inside and outside myself at the same time?

As Viktor Shklovsky suggested later, the people at the Stray Dog knew, somewhere inside themselves, that revolution was imminent, but they also felt as if they were somehow located outside of time and space, as if nothing in what others saw as reality could actually touch them. Then, of course, the reality they didn't believe in came along and one by one devoured them. The poet is not the author. The poet is the subject.

Joseph Brodsky, attempting to understand why Akhmatova's son was so angry at her, spoke of the dissonance between the sufferer and the writer, suggests that the poet submits to the demands of the muse, the poem being a greater truth than the truth of experience. But one pays for this. To be loyal to art, you sin against the ordinary truth, and against your own pain.

I bring you knowledge of Death. Take a last look at everything and say goodbye to it.

Ghosts enter in the masks of mummers. The room is a hall of mirrors. Don Juan and Faust are puppets. A woman steps out of a portrait. I don't want to meet the person I asked to be. A room full of jewels and bones.

Olga and Khlebnikov are both obsessed with birds. She dances like a bird. He sees her as a frail little bird. Olga's husband painted birds on the walls. Flight.

In her old age, Akhmatova thought the careless infidelities of the Stray Dog were a corruption of the soul. Echoes of Four Quartets in her work. Pasternak had given her a copy. The future ripening into the past.

Mayakovsky, like a rocket in a yellow shirt. A primitive, elemental force, like a storm. Bigger than life. A Prehistoric man from the future. All this damned pretending. In Tashkent, the camel spoke to me in Russian.

Lermontov: The Demon. Tries to find salvation from Nihilism with love for Tamara. But his kiss destroys her. An angel takes her soul to heaven. Vrubel's painting.

Where is Meyerhold? What's happened to Meyerhold? Meyerhold's theatre: stimulation and fragmentation. Music hall and circus. Mystery plays. Farces. Carnivals. Acrobats. Jugglers. Clowns. The Director is God, and he is dead.

If the song is sung honestly, everything else vanishes. There is only space, the stars, and the singer. I didn't care about the shooting. I wanted to see everything. There was blood in the snow.

It was a good house to play hide and seek in, said Tamara. Except when they'd go off and abandon you. There was always a sense of lurking terror. A red haired angel waiting to carry me off. A dream of a house full of many rooms. I'd walk through rooms and down corridors. Something after me, or me after something. It's all a game of hide and seek. The pale man comes for me.

I don't need much happiness. I am fashionably rude. I have betrayed you.

Before science, said Nedobrovo, people thought in images. A play is an induced hallucination.

Akhmatova was born near Odessa, in the Ukraine, of a Ukrainian father and a Russian mother. She grew up in Tsarskoye Selo, near St Petersburg, and, like Tsvetayeva, was haunted by Pushkin. She loved roses, music and Shakespeare. Every summer they returned to the Black Sea. She could climb trees like a squirrel.

A play made of intersecting triangles.

In this place, Gogol said, the Devil lights the lamps so everything will look like what it's not. Visiting us, who stained the earth with blood. We are one in Hell, as we were above. We each create our own Hell.

The moon leers down like a drunkard. In my dream I sent her a black rose. The statue of the Tsar is coming to drag me down to Hell. I kissed her hands and shoulders. I took her home, but she turned out to be made of cardboard. Something flew out of the mirrors.

Meyerhold saw his experiments not as just a stylistic choice. He saw the grotesque elements in his productions as a representation of the irrational and the mysterious at the core of experience. I'm with him on this. Part of his problem with Stanislavsky was that he thought Stanislavsky's methods were excessively rational, which human experience is not. He tried to explain what is inexplicable instead of just showing it. It is rational to ask an actor to come up with a motive for any given thing he says or does onstage, but it is not much like experience. It is the utter, irrational strangeness inherent in experience that Meyerhold was interested in. I'm with him on that, too. But about character, I think Meyerhold had a profound phobia about emotion and Stanislavsky was right.

Meyerhold turns everybody into puppets, and so does the state, says Brik. You're terrified of the truth. So you hide in the theatre. Puppets and clowns. Dehumanized people. Masks. Now we must all wear masks.

I carried her off in a sleigh, but she turned into a cardboard doll.

When we make a measurement, we are not seeing reality. We are seeing what we can measure. Every observation is about the act of observation, and every observer is complicit in what he observes. The moment the audience starts watching, they have made themselves a part of the action.

The whole theatre is the café. The audience is sitting at tables and is surrounded by the play. It is Anna's hallucination in 1941, so it must be anachronistic, like a shuffled pack of cards. An accordion. A cello. A tambourine. Clowns. Puppets. A man in a bear suit. A giant nose appears, sits and has a drink with the bear. Tolstoy's ghost appears. He is there to condemn them as self-indulgent and deluded.

If you really loved me, you'd love the way I smell.

Nobody can love the way you smell.

Then nobody can love me.

Don't feel bad. Nobody can love anybody. Nobody you love is real. Nobody is real.

The person who kills you is real.

What if the person who kills you is the person you love?

It doesn't matter because you're dead.

I am sick of the squeezed lemons and picked chicken bones of the little world of the liberal mystic intelligentsia. The way of mystery and the way of theatre do not merge. Bring in the meat puppets.

Terrifying, said Mandelstam, to realize that our life is a tale without a hero, without a plot, made up of desolation, out of the feverish babble of unending digressions, out of the delirium of influenza.

Clowns sit at the table. Another table is full of puppets. A bear walks through a puppet show. Red lights on snow. We are all winter people here.

Directing, Meyerhold was all over the place, running on and off the stage, watching from the first row or one back. Like him, I prefer a steeply raked auditorium, not a raked stage.

When Stanislavsky died in August of 1938, he said, take care of Meyerhold. He is my only heir here or anywhere.

There are Babylonian cuneiform tablets in the garbage. To study ancient civilizations is to realize that your own civilization is as mortal as you are.

Giordano Bruno said that in a universe where God exists, all opposites must eventually merge.

It was all the tapping of a branch
on a windowpane.
The blood black carnival goes on,
even in the rain.

This is secret writing, the cryptogram of a forbidden method. A lantern and a bunch of keys, emissaries from the Noseless Slut.

Our separation is imaginary. My shadow stains your walls like mold. You bring confusion to my dreams. Reality emerging from the mirror.

We are already on the other side of hell. Please do not try to stand up in the boat.

This makes no sense. You don't know who loves whom, who met whom when, and why, who died and who lived, who the author is, who is the hero. What do we need with a confused sermon about a poet and a swarm of ghosts?

This is why I let the birds fly free in my apartment.

Objects, when paid attention to, take on unexpected significance.

Why did Akhmatova always feel a lingering sense of guilt about Knyazev's suicide over Olga? Because he came to her for comfort and what she said to him might have pushed him over the edge? Did she tell him Olga was sleeping with Blok? Why would she do that? Her own unhappiness over Gumilyov and Kutuzov? She had married Gumilyov only after he tried to kill himself twice over her. Later, observing his numerous infidelities, did she suspect it was all a trick? Or did she resent the fascination that Olga held for Gumilyov and all of the men at the Stray Dog? Or was she a bit in love with Olga herself? Complex psychological reasons, mostly buried in her, that she could never completely understand. Olga is dancing with Rasputin's head.

Lily and Rasputin on the train. Somehow, it haunts her. Why does she find evil so attractive? We are not to tell fortunes with Tatyana. But of course, we can't resist.

When Marinetti the Futurist visited the Stray Dog in 1913, Artur Lurye gave a talk on the art of noise. Later, in the summer of 1921, Lurye invited Akhmatova to join him and Olga Sudeikina in their flat on the Fontanka. Anna left the Babylonian and joined them. Lurye and Olga were lovers, and Lurye and Anna were lovers. Some have also speculated that Anna and Olga were lovers, but others think that would have been completely out of character for Anna, if not for Olga.

But different observers reported that Akhmatova might have had Lesbian relations or inclinations, not just with Olga, but also with the actress Ranevskaya, and with Ostrovskaya. She is described as having an erect, queenly air, enhanced by her austere beauty, but she could also be gossipy, sarcastic and a bit malicious. Olga often threatened suicide. When she had pneumonia, in the summer of 1924, Anna nursed her. When Olga moved to Paris, she left some of her dolls with Anna. She referred to Olga as her double.

Fucking her in the observatory while all above us the universe turns like a carousel. What does it matter what you write down and what is forgotten? Mars looking down through the trees at the dead man looking up. In Apple Tree Yard at the World's End.

Half a harlot, half a nun. Now the calumny's begun.

Terror, fingering things in the dark.

Eyes of the lynx. Burning my notebooks at the edge of the sea. Sound of a doorbell ringing. Don't answer it. It's the Devil. Sometimes the best poem is silence.

The nodes of the triangles are what links one scene to the next. A person from one triangle is also a node on another triangle, and this is our path through the labyrinth.

Mandelstam introduced Akhmatova to Mayakovsky at the Stray Dog. We are like *Dead Souls*. An assemblage of martyrs.

One who knows too much grows old too soon. We were poor but happy, said Tamara. I used to collect fungus and keep it for a pet. I would pretend that I lived in my doll house. I was a doll who was kidnapped by Gypsies.

Akhmatova loved Bach and Vivaldi, Leopardi and Mistral, and could drink like a storm trooper without seeming drunk.

I was born on Midsummer night. I have fairy powers. Wood nymph powers. I am different with everybody. I am many people. I am the picture of Nobody. I get telephone calls from the dead.

This is done to please the fool and death. Where am I? What world is this? Is this not strange? When I was born, the wind was north-northwest.' And yet the plot is the one thing we know. Walking on broken glass. Please go away. Please go. Please stay. We can't make up our minds. No matter which way you turn, it comes out crooked. Draped in cobwebs. To give back the dust one has borrowed.

Theatre is a means of inducing a trance. God is all possible combinations of events.

I once fought a duel over a woman, said Gumilyov. I said something crude about her, and some idiot felt he had to defend her honor, which was a figment of his imagination to begin with. We met where D'Anthes killed Pushkin. Alexey Tolstoy stepped into a huge puddle and disappeared up to his hat. I shot and missed. The other fellow was too terrified to pull the trigger, so finally Alexey, who was freezing to death, took the gun away from him and shot into the ground, and we all went home. The only thing in the world more ridiculous than a woman is a man.

This is the second death. Even the lake of fire. We are one in Hell, even as we were above. Abandon all hope. I am the ferryman of dead souls. We are the damned. We are not permitted to repent. We have each freely chosen our own private hell. Christmas trees burning in the forest. And the eyes of wolves glaring into the darkness. Mounds of human heads. God laughing. Why has the music stopped? Why this overwhelming silence?

Last night I dreamed that Tolstoy's ghost came to warn me of something. But I can't make out what it is.

Tolstoy's Ghost, appearing from out of the snow, in eerie blue light: Shame on you. Shame on you all. It's disgraceful, what you do here. Fucking each other like a bunch of goats. And what is all this damned smoke? I can't see anything. What am I doing in this place? Is this Hell? Have I ended up in Hell? Or is it just somebody's cellar? Everything is darkness. Like pigs to the slaughter. In a universe where God exists, all opposites must eventually merge. Kicked about like a rotten old parsnip. This is excessive suckage. It was all the tapping of a dead branch on the windowpane. If this vulgar behavior continues, Russia is doomed.

Here at the Stray Dog, we play Debussy and Ragtime, both at the same time. Is this the beginning of something or the end of something? Yes.

Why shouldn't I publish his poems? Mayakovsky is a genius. I know because he told me so himself. I am much more intelligent, but he's a genius. There is a huge ocean of sorrow in between.

Shklovsky said, Lily looked at Mayakovsky as if he were not quite tamed lightning.

The dead lie in the streets. A wrought iron lamp on cobblestones. The wind tears through the city, ripping posters from the walls. The river flows backwards.

For Meyerhold it wasn't just body control. It was emotional control. One was to display emotions only in a controlled, formal way. Intelligence and self control. Pavlov and the Behaviorists. Dangerous and ultimately stupid company.

Blok began as a mystical idealist, but gradually grew more cynical, was briefly excited by the revolution, but in the end came to have serious doubts about the ability of human beings to be constant in love, and about whether or not any person actually has a coherent identity. Here, he said, nobody knows how to love.

What do you want?
To be with you in Hell.

30 Dec 1906: Meyerhold directs Blok's Puppet Show at Komisarzhevskaya's theatre.

Everything has died. Nothing has remained.

Some loves of Anna: Lurye, Punin, Nedebrovo, Anrep, Shileiko. She met Anrep Lent 1915. He was the mosaic artist she speaks of. Shileiko was the Assyriologist, Lurye the musician, Punin the art critic. All of them made her very unhappy.

Creation means sacrifice. God sacrifices himself and becomes the world. Then the world becomes God. This is lila, the play of God. God is a playwright magician who transforms himself into the world through the magical act of creation. This is what maya means. When, deep under this magic spell, we confuse God's play with reality, we are lost in appearances. Creation is magic.

What we observe, said Heisenberg, is not nature itself, but nature exposed to our method of questioning.

Everything contains within it the seed of its opposite, like the dots in the yin yang symbol. The recognition of this is what irony is. Returning is the nature of the Tao, said Lao Tzu. Going far means returning.

Prospero on his island. A wax candle burns in the bedroom. The guest from behind the mirror. The terrible chaos of the past. Bloodstained kisses.

Energy is time, said the maniac in the street. Mass is space. Mass is concentrated in energy. Space is concentrated in time. Particles are probability patterns. We are made of particles. We are made of probability patterns. Every particle is a process.

Put the light out and open the door. Take whatever shape you choose. An old woman howling like an animal.

Hovering on the borderline of delirium and hallucination. It was like this in Babylon before aliens from the Red Planet descended upon them, promising unlimited meatballs.

Love reveals itself in fits of despair and irony. Careening wildly down the wrong road.

Lyubov had long blond hair. A 300 year old oak tree and orchard. She and Blok both loved the theatre, and in many ways were only happy there.

Verses to the beautiful lady. Fireflies in the darkness. Sirius and Vega, shining down on a summer night. You were Hamlet, she said. I was Ophelia. Wild strawberries.

In Meyerhold's film of *The Picture Of Dorian Gray*, Dorian (played by a young woman) takes Lord Henry (a sinister Meyerhold) to see Sybil play Juliet. We never see the stage directly. On the wall behind Lord Henry's box is a tall mirror in which we can see reflected the balcony scene. So we can see the scene itself, reflected behind them in the mirror, and the two onlookers, reacting to the scene as it happens. This is very revealing of Meyerhold's approach to things. It is the strategy of indirect approach. But later, he loses some of this, caught up in propaganda.

It's too early to pity the enemy, said Brik. First you've got to finish him off.

On the train to his exile and death, Mandelstam stares out the window at the snow.

Meyerhold thought the entire creative act should be a conscious process. But the problem is, it's not, and any attempt to force it to be that is likely to result in ultimate falseness and sterility. He does return to the idea of rousing emotion by creating physical points of excitation that are informed with some particular emotion, trusting that this somehow will grip the audience. But he wants to get to emotion through a combination of physicality and intellect. That, from my point of view, is grabbing the mule the wrong end round. With Meyerhold, in large measure, I think it's about control. He doesn't trust emotion, often with good reason.

It's one thing to dismember, adapt and reconstruct the classics. The classics can generally take care of themselves. The texts are easily available to everybody. It's quite another thing to dismember the work of a living playwright. There is no way for the audience to tell the play from what the director has done with it. In the hands of a genius like Meyerhold, the result might in fact end up being more interesting than a more straightforward presentation of the text. But the result of this sort of tampering is more often an arrogant mess, mostly about the director's ego. This is one reason copyright is so important. Without a strong copyright law to protect the author, the profession of self-employed writer can't really exist. At best one would have to spend most of one's time doing something else, just to earn a living so that we could write in stolen hours. The author's right to decide what is and is not part of the work of art they've created is absolutely essential to the survival of art in a free society. Meyerhold was ruthless about ignoring the author's wishes when it suited him, and since there was no real protection for the author in Soviet Russia, he could get away with it, with sometimes decidedly unspectacular results. But when Stalin decided Meyerhold was a threat, he himself rewrote the play of Meyerhold's life. Russia was Stalin's theatre, and all the actors were slaves. Anybody who objected was simply written out of the play.

Soviet censors rejecting Erdman's *The Suicide* said: "It is necessary to experiment in the theatrical form, but experiment in politics is not permissible." Meyerhold produced it anyway. Stalin's vicious henchman Kaganovich came, and sat in the front row. At a critical moment in the play, the actor Ilinsky, as Meyerhold had directed, offered up a revolver to Kaganovich and his party, who recoiled in horror, with the clear suggesting that Kaganovich was welcome to shoot himself with it. Ilinsky then put it on the floor and pushed it towards him with his foot. Please, he said. Help yourself. From that moment on, Meyerhold probably knew he was doomed. Erdman was arrested and sent to Siberia. He never completed another full length play. And not long after, Meyerhold was arrested, tortured, and shot.

Bely said, Dreams. Nothing but dreams. He was fascinated by entropy. At the end of his life, Nadezhda Mandelstam said, Bely collected pebbles and leaves and made complicated patterns with them.

Hurdy gurdy music with clowns. Hit with a sack of billiard balls.

It should be noted that much of what we are seeing here happened at different times and places, not in the Stray Dog. The Blok-Lyubov-Bely relationship had its most intense period before the Stray Dog. And Mochulsky seems to assert that Blok never went to the Stray Dog at all. It seems fairly clear that he never read his work there, but I don't know that it's been proven he never once set foot there. In any case, what we are seeing is Akhmatova's hallucinatory dream-vision of her life from about 1910 to 1940. The Stray Dog is, spiritually, the place where the greatest Russian writers and artists, musicians and theatre folk, come together in her head. It is a place where imagined and half-remembered fragments coalesce. The mosaic is made of many small pieces.

Blok was happiest in a big, empty theatre, watching *King Lear* rehearse, perhaps. As he grew older and sicker, he wanted Lyubov to be there more and more.

Mandelstam said, Expect nothing and be ready for anything. That's the key to not losing one's mind. But I am losing my mind.

Pasternak told a friend that going to visit the Briks had become an increasingly uncomfortable experience for him. Brik was often out with his friends in the Secret Police. Brik described his experiences there as a good way for a man to lose his sentimentality, and then described several grisly episodes as examples. Eventually, Pasternak found Brik repulsive. He said working with the Secret Police had ruined him. There is no evidence that Brik was there when Meyerhold was interrogated, tortured and murdered, but it seems clear that he had been present at such things. There is also no hard evidence that he was assigned to spy on Mayakovsky, but it seems to me very unlikely that he would not have reported what was going on with him to his Cheka friends.

Art is mystical, says Blok, but not religious. He suffered from the contagion of mystical irony. I have abandoned nihilism, he said, but there is much stupidity and filth in my head.

Akhmatova believed she was descended from Genghis Khan.

Enigmatic correspondences. Blue snow is falling. Ecstatic states of the soul.

Nadezhda Mandelstam tells of a conversation she had with a member of the Secret Police about his first assignment. He was told to stand outside an old man's house and make note of anybody who entered or left. The problem was, nobody ever came to see the old man, and the old man never left the building. Every once in a while the spy would see a curtain pulled back from the window, and the old man peering out at him. Then one night a horrible suspicion took possession of him: what if the old man was actually assigned to spy on me?

TIME LINE

1799   Pushkin born.
1809   Gogol born.
1818   Turgenev born.
1821   Dostoyevsky born.
1828   Tolstoy born.
1837   Pushkin shot in duel, dies.
1852   Gogol burns second part of *Dead Souls*, starves himself to death.
1860   Chekhov born.
1863   Stanislavsky born.
1868   Gorky born.
1869   Rasputin born.
1874   Meyerhold born.
1878   Stalin born.
1880   Blok born. Bely born.
1881   Dostoyevsky dies. Lyubov Blok born.
1883   Turgenev dies.
1885   Karsavina born. Olga Glebova-Sudeikina born.
1886   Nikolai Gumilyov born.
1888   Osip Brik born.
1889   Anna Akhmatova born near Odessa.
1890   Pasternak born.
1891   Lily Brik born. Mandelstam born. Bulgakov born.
1892   Tsvetayeva born.
1893   Mayakovsky born.
1894   Zinaida Raikh born.
1895   Sergey Yesenin born. Meyerhold plays the Murderer.
1900   Anna begins writing poetry.
1903   Anna meets Gumilyov, and he begins courting her.
1904   Chekhov dies.
1905   Japanese destroy Russian fleet. First revolution. Anna's parents separate.

1907   Anna's first poem published by Gumilyov. She rejects his marriage proposal.

1909   Anna agrees to marry Gumilyov.

1910   Tolstoy dies. Akhmatova marries Gumilyov. Honeymoon in Paris. Gumilyov travels to mideast.

1911   Gumilyov returns. Pronin opens Stray Dog Café. Gumilyov, Akhmatova and Mandelstam break with Symbolists, call themselves Acmeists.

1912   Anna's first collection of poems published. Son born.

1913   29 March Knyazev shoots himself. Dies 5 April. Gumilyov goes to Abyssinia.

1914   Rasputin murdered. War begins. Gumilyov volunteers, sent to front.

1915   Lily meets Mayakovsky. Gorky hears Mayakovsky read at the Stray Dog. Mayakovsky reads "The Cloud In Trousers" for the Briks, and they fall in love with him. Anna's father dies.

1916   Anna meets Boris Anrep.

1917   Yesenin marries Zinaida Raikh. Revolution. Kerensky's provisional government. Lenin seizes power in October.

1918   Akhmatova divorces Gumilyov, marries Assyrian scholar Shileiko.

1919   Red Terror against opponents of Soviet regime begins.

1920   Anna separates from Shileiko.

1921   Anna goes to live with Olga. 7 Aug Blok dies. 25 Aug Gumilyov is shot.

1922   Mayakovsky publicly denounces Anna's poetry. Khlebnikov starves to death.

1924   Akhmatova living with Olga. Death of Lenin. Emergence of Stalin. Mandelstam introduces Anna to his wife Nadezhda. Olga moves to Paris. Anna seeing art historian Nikolay Punin.

1925   Yesenin's suicide. Anna's poems refused publication from now until 1940. Anna lives with Nadezhda, both ill with tuberculosis.

1926   Anna and Shileiko divorce. She moves in with Punin and wife.

1929   Meyerhold produces Mayakovsky's *The Bedbug.*

1930   Meyerhold produces Mayakovsky's *The Bath House.* 14 Apr Mayakovsky shoots himself in the chest. Age 36.

1933   Anna living with Bulgakovs and Mandelstams in Moscow. Son arrested, released.

1934   8 Jan Bely dies. 13 May Mandelstam arrested. Mandelstam's exiled. Anna collects money for them from friends. Mass arrests. Stalinist terror.

1935   Son and Punin arrested, then released.

1936   Gorky dies.

1937   Millions of Russians arrested and sent to concentration camps.

1938   Son arrested. Aug Stanislavsky dies. Anna separates from Punin. 27 Dec Mandelstam dies in transit camp.

1939   Lyubov Blok dies. Tsvetayeva returns to Russia. June: Meyerhold and wife Zinaida Raikh arrested. Later, she's released. 17 July Zinaida Raikh found dead in flat, 11 knife wounds, throat cut. .

1940   1 Feb Secret trial of Meyerhold. 2 Feb Meyerhold shot. Ban on Anna's poems lifted, but publication of new book halted on orders from Stalin. Bulgakov dies.

1941   Tsvetayeva and Anna meet. Marina Tsvetayeva hangs herself. Siege of Leningrad. Anna and Tomashevsky stumble into cellar and realize it was the Stray Dog.

1945   22 Feb Osip Brik dies. Isaiah Berlin visits Anna in Leningrad. Olga dies.

1946   Anna publicly condemned by Central Committee and expelled from Union of Soviet Writers.

1953   Stalin dies.
1960   Pasternak dies.
1966   5 Mar Anna Akhmatova dies.
1978   Karsavina dies.
        Lily Brik dies.

My Little Russian Sweetheart

Music and Lyrics:
Don Nigro

Come to me, my lit - tle Rus - sian sweet - heart.

Let me hold you now be - fore the dawn.

Soon e - nough we will both be for - got - ten.
Soon e - nough we will all be for - got - ten.

Time will stop, and then it will move on.
Time will stop, and we will all be gone.